To: Joc Arnaud
From: Rosalyn Oakley
Re: *Our* Potential Baby

Joc,

As you know, the results of my pregnancy test will appear shortly. You have your list of demands, should a pink line appear. I have mine:

1: The baby will be an Oakley and have *my* name. Oakleys have deep roots in these parts. Roots are important to *me*.

2: The baby will grow up on *my* ranch—which by the way, I will never sell to you!—not your gated palace.

3: You will not tell me what to do.

Sincerely,

Rosalyn OAKLEY

Dear Reader,

You met Joc Arnaud as a minor character in *The Prince's Mistress,* where he "negotiated" a marriage contract between his sister, Ana, and Prince Lander Montgomery. Lander warned Joc that the time would come when Joc would find himself in a similar situation. "Someday you'll find yourself boxed into a corner like this. Remember me when that happens, Arnaud. Remember, and know that you brought it on yourself when you forced this agreement on the one woman you should have protected, and the one man who will do whatever it takes to see that you pay for your arrogance."

Well, that time has come and Joc is thrust into the negotiation of his life.

I love stories that put characters into tight spots and force them to make tough decisions. It strips them down to the bare essence of who they are and what they want—and what lengths they'll go to obtain that ultimate desire. Stories like those make me wonder…what's most important in our lives? And what extremes will we go to gain what we want most?

For more information about my latest releases, please visit me at my Web site: www.dayleclaire.com. I love hearing from readers!

Best,

Day

DAY LECLAIRE

THE BILLIONAIRE'S BABY NEGOTIATION

Published by Silhouette Books
America's Publisher of Contemporary Romance

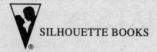

SILHOUETTE BOOKS

ISBN-13: 978-0-373-76821-9
ISBN-10:   0-373-76821-4

THE BILLIONAIRE'S BABY NEGOTIATION

Books by Day Leclaire

Silhouette Desire

*The Forbidden Princess #1780
*The Prince's Mistress #1786
*The Royal Wedding Night #1792
The Billionaire's Baby Negotiation #1821

*The Royals

DAY LECLAIRE

is a multi-award-winning author of nearly forty novels. Her passionate books offer a unique combination of humor, emotion and unforgettable characters, which have won Day tremendous worldwide popularity, as well as numerous publishing honors. She is a three-time winner of both the Colorado Award of Excellence and the Golden Quill Award. She's won *Romantic Times BOOKreviews* magazine's Career Achievement, and Love and Laughter Awards, a Holt Medallion, a Booksellers Best Award, and she has received an impressive ten nominations for the prestigious Romance Writers of America RITA® Award.

Day's romances touch the heart and make you care about her characters as much as she does. In Day's own words, "I adore writing romances and can't think of a better way to spend each day."

To Hazen F. Totton. Thanks, Mom!
You're always there when I need you most.

One

Enough was enough! One way or another all this nonsense ended today.

Rosalyn Oakley approached the pair of gigantic double wooden doors leading to Joc Arnaud's inner sanctum and paused to gather her self-control. She wiped her damp palms on the seat of her jeans. *Steady.* She could do this. She just needed to remember how much was at stake. Security wouldn't have let her get this far if Arnaud hadn't approved it. A humorless smile touched her mouth. Maybe he was as curious to meet the one woman who refused to cave to his demands, as she was to meet the one man who never gave up.

The thought helped fortify her, and she thrust open the doors and stepped into Arnaud's conference room and into another world. An endless sweep of tinted glass surrounded her, offering a dazzling panoramic view of the city of Dallas. Heat and humidity shimmered on the far side of the windows, while inside all remained cool and quiet and rich.

Rich in possessions. Rich in design. Rich with people.

An inlaid conference table stretched before her, the strips of wood that made up the surface a kaleidoscope of type and color. The craftsman had employed every variety of wood imaginable from a deep masculine mahogany to the blush white of red oak to the plummy tones of cherry. She sensed a design present, but didn't have the opportunity to examine the table, not with the several dozen people seated around the circumference, their papers littering the surface.

At her advent, all eyes swiveled to clash with hers and she took a moment to sweep her gaze over each person in an attempt to identify which was Arnaud. For an instant she keyed in on the person seated at the head of the table before dismissing him. And then she noticed the man standing to one side of the room, leaning against a sideboard, steaming coffee cup in hand. She focused her attention on him.

Business Executive was written all over him, from the tips of his Gucci shoes to the black Armani suit stretched across impressive, broad shoulders. He topped her by a full nine or ten inches, every one of his sculpted inches packed with lean, solid muscle. She tilted her head back and peered out from beneath the brim of her Stetson. His height forced her to look a long way up to meet his gaze, and put her at an instant disadvantage.

Deep-set obsidian eyes stared at her from one of the

most striking faces she'd ever seen. Lean and golden, with high, sharp cheekbones, the blood of his Native American ancestors had left an indelible stamp on that impressive bone structure. His hair was black and longer than conventional, which surprised her considering this had to be Joc Arnaud—the top honcho.

He returned her look with an open once-over that felt less offensive than something more discreet. He lifted a sooty eyebrow. "Lost your way?"

"On the contrary. I just found it." She approached him. "Do you know who I am?"

"Rosalyn Oakley," he answered promptly. "Age, twenty-eight. Born April 5. One hundred eighteen pounds. Sole heir to Longhorn Ranch." A hard smile flitted across his mouth. "Which, I believe, is where I come in. You own the ranch. I want it."

His swift summation of the facts threw her off stride, no doubt the purpose of his little recital. She recovered with all due speed, getting straight to the point. "Your two henchmen just paid me a visit. I'm returning the favor." She spared a glance at the suits-and-ties grouped around the conference table, who were listening with avid curiosity. She jerked her head in their direction. "You want to do this in public? Or would you rather we settle our differences in private?"

Without taking his gaze from her, he issued a single word, "Out."

There was a dignified scramble after that, one that would have left Rosalyn laughing if the circumstances had been different. The instant the door closed behind the final underling, she squared off against him. She'd spent the entire trip into Dallas planning what she'd say and she gave him chapter and verse in a single, direct volley.

"You've approached me—or rather your employees have approached me—about selling my ranch to you. And I've been civil with them each time they've turned up on my doorstep. I've told them no as clearly and politely as I know how. But it's gotten to the point where I can't turn around without tripping over them. It's going to stop and you're going to make it stop."

To her dismay, the only change in his expression was a deepening intensity in the way he watched her, and a slight smile that added immense appeal to an all-too attractive face. The distraction cost her. It took her a split second to remember where she'd left off in her script and get back on point.

"Anyway," she continued doggedly, "I've come to tell you in person that I'm not selling, in the hopes that you'll finally get the message and leave me alone. I don't care what you do, I don't care how many thugs you send, I'm not leaving my land."

At the end of her recital, he returned his coffee cup to the sideboard and faced her. She could tell from his expression she wouldn't like his response. Before he could speak, a discreet buzz emanated from a nearby phone. With a brief apology, he took the call. "No interruptions," he said without preamble. He listened for an instant before grimacing, then glanced at Rosalyn and said, "This will only take a minute."

"Do you want me to wait outside?" She hated making the offer, but common courtesy had been bred into her bones.

He shook his head, before addressing the caller. "Hello, MacKenzie. What can I do for my least favorite sister?"

Rosalyn could hear the furious blast from clear across the room and winced. Someone wasn't happy.

"Sorry. Half sister. Is that better?" Apparently it wasn't, because the angry diatribe continued until he cut it off. "Unless I'm mistaken, you've called to ask me a favor. Instead of bringing up old history, I suggest you get to it."

He listened at length and Rosalyn shivered at the cold bitterness of his expression. Is that how he really felt toward his sister? She didn't understand it. So what if they were half siblings? Family was family was family. Something hideous must have happened between them to cause this serious a rift.

"I'm not selling it, MacKenzie, and that's final. Your mother sold the property to me, and if you're not happy with Meredith's decision, I suggest you take it up with her." A wintry smile swept across his face. "At least you and my brothers—excuse me, half brothers—can comfort yourselves knowing it's still in the family, even if it's the illegitimate branch."

With that he hung up. Though he appeared calm and collected on the surface, she observed a raw quality gnawing at the edges of his restraint, a ferocity struggling for expression. He focused his inky gaze on her and she met it head-on. Slowly the anger eased and when he spoke it was with impressive composure. "Why don't we start over and do this the right way?" He held out his hand. "Joc Arnaud."

She hesitated a brief second. Unable to help herself, she offered her hand in return. "Rosalyn Oakley."

He captured her in his grasp and suddenly the spacious conference room became a suffocating box. Everything about him overwhelmed her. His grip. The dichotomy of callused fingers and palm attached to the hand of a white-collar exec. His size. His innate power. Even the crisp, masculine scent that clung to him invaded her senses and threatened to rob her of her will.

It became hard to breathe, let alone think, especially when he stood so close. She shouldn't have this sort of physical reaction to a complete stranger, especially when that stranger was her worst nightmare. Unfortunately he'd just proven beyond all doubt that she had no control whatsoever over her visceral response to him. Maybe it would have been easier if he weren't so drop-dead gorgeous. And even though she'd handled gorgeous on occasion in the past, one small problem tripped her up when it came to this man.

The face.

This particular face was organized into a masculine toughness, the sort that had most men maintaining a wary distance while women stumbled over themselves to get closer. It also happened to be the most attractive— not to mention dangerous—of all the faces she'd ever encountered. Worse, underpinning his toughness was a blatant appraisal, almost sexual in nature, that challenged her on some instinctive level.

What had she been told about this man? Black eyes, black hair, black heart. Why, oh why, hadn't anyone warned her about the equally black desire he could arouse with one simple touch?

He continued to hold her hand in his. "Let's start

from the top," he suggested. "I want to buy Longhorn Ranch. What will it take to make that to happen?"

That one question freed her from his spell and had her tugging her hand from his grasp. She managed to resist the urge to wipe her palm against her jeans—just—and took a swift step backward to give herself some breathing room. She didn't care if her retreat gave him a slight edge in whatever game he'd set in motion. Distance was more important right now than gaining a negotiating advantage.

"I'll make this easy for you, Arnaud. I won't sell."

He swept her claim aside as though it were inconsequential. Maybe in his book it was. "I don't think you understand. I win. Always. No matter what it takes."

A chill shot up her spine and she fought to keep the apprehension from showing in her expression. "Not this time."

"Every time." He folded his arms across his chest. "Now explain it to me. Why are you being so stubborn? I've offered you a generous price, haven't I?"

She stared at him in disbelief. Whipping off her hat in a "getting down to business" gesture, she tossed it toward the empty conference table where it landed with a soft thud. "This isn't about money! That land has been in my family since before Texas became a state. The only way I leave it is in a box." She tilted her head to one side. "Is that how you plan to steal it away from me, Arnaud? Do your goons take matters that far, or are they limited to simple threats and warnings?"

"I've never resorted to physical violence." A frown crept across his face. "Have they touched you? Harmed you in any way?"

"Neither of them has actually touched me, but—" She shrugged, remembering the implied threat in both word and look. "Men like that say a lot without saying a lot, if you understand what I mean."

"I'll take care of it. Violence is never necessary. Why would it be? Everyone has a price." His expression grew knowing. "What's yours?"

"There is no price," she insisted.

A hint of amusement gleamed in the rich darkness of his eyes. "Of course there is. You just don't realize it, yet. But I'll find your weakness. And when I do, you'll sell."

He shot her a smile and she froze. How was it that with one simple smile he could melt all that was most feminine in her, while at the same time turning her blood to ice? It was like confronting a grizzly. One was awed by the power and beauty of the animal, wanting to somehow embrace such magnificence, while at the same time knowing that one did so at their own peril. One swipe of his paw, and the bear could end your existence.

She swallowed. Hard. "And if I don't sell? What then?"

"I up the ante until you do."

"And if that doesn't work?"

Anxiety had her voice growing soft and unsteady. Damn it! She couldn't afford to show this man any hint of weakness. Based on his expression, she'd done precisely that. Great. Just great. Now that he'd picked up on her vulnerability, he'd never back down.

His smile flashed again, unnerving her. "There's always a way to get what I want if I'm patient. It's a matter of finding which option will work best. I keep trying different ones until I find the right lever." He took a step in her direction, that single stride bringing him to within a foot of where she stood. "I don't suppose you'd care to tell me which lever would work best with you?"

He was too close. Far too close. More than anything, she wanted to fall back another pace. Instead she dug in her heels. "I'd rather not." She folded her arms across her chest. "So you're not going to call off your goons? You're going to keep harassing me?"

"I'll call them off. They won't bother you again, I promise. As for harassing you…" He dismissed the suggestion with a shake of his head. "That's such a negative word. I prefer to think of it as getting better acquainted."

She blinked at that. "Why would you want to get better acquainted? Why would I, for that matter?"

He appeared surprised by the question. "So you'll be in a better position to negotiate, of course."

Enough was enough. "I'm not interested in getting to know you any better than I'd want to become better acquainted with a rattlesnake. I don't negotiate with them any more than I would with you."

He lifted an eyebrow, clearly intrigued. "Off with their heads?"

"If that's what it takes. As for you, well… Everyone has a price." She parroted his own words back to him. "Even you. You just don't realize it, yet. But I'll find your weakness. And when I do, you'll go away. Permanently."

She'd said all she needed to. Coming here had been pointless. It was clear Arnaud wouldn't give up on trying to buy her land. That didn't mean she had to sell. He seemed to think he had something she wanted. He didn't.

There was nothing she wanted or needed that she didn't already have. The sooner he realized that, the better.

She spun on her heel and marched toward the door. Her gaze shifted to the table as she passed it and what she saw almost had her breaking stride. Without all the papers to clutter the surface she could make out the design of the inlaid wood—a huge, magnificent wolf.

Her analogy had been dead wrong. Arnaud wasn't a grizzly, but a timber wolf. She'd seen one once, had been riveted by the keen intelligence glittering in its golden eyes. A loner. A predator. Proud and protective. She could understand why the animal had been deified by various cultures over the millennia. She didn't dare look back at Arnaud. But an acute awareness filled her.

She'd just pitted herself against the legendary Big Bad, himself. And unlike in fairy tales, this particular wolf didn't lose.

Joc watched Rosalyn cross to the far side of the room, her stride long and loose. It spoke of a woman comfortable in her own skin. He also saw her glance at the table and the hitch in her step when she caught a glimpse of the wolf motif. He smiled at that telling reaction, amused all the more by the fact that his table had intimidated her more than he had.

She reached the exit and stood there for a split second as she opened the door, captured by the morning sunlight filtering in through the windows. It embraced her with its heavy rays and set her hair on fire. The view held him spellbound. Well, hell. He'd roped himself a redhead, the red so deep and rich he hadn't noticed it until the sun had betrayed her secret. The instant she left the room, he pushed a button in the console by his chair.

"Yes, Mr. Arnaud?"

"Lock down the elevators."

"Right away, Mr. Arnaud."

Joc crossed to the end of the table and picked up the hat Rosalyn had forgotten to retrieve on her way out the door, no doubt because she'd been knocked off-kilter by the wolf design. The Stetson had seen serious wear. It was the hat of a working rancher, not an accessory to demonstrate state pride or as a fashion statement, but for vital protection against the elements. It told him a lot about its owner…and how he might handle her.

He left the conference room and started toward the elevators. His executive assistant's desk was on the way and he paused long enough to give Maggie a list of instructions and have her release the elevators. That done, he tracked down Rosalyn.

He found her stabbing at the button for the elevator. Joc slowed, taking the time to study her. He'd had the impression of height when they'd talked, a false impression he realized now. Maybe it had been her subtle perfume that had distracted him, or the striking shade of her Texas Bluebonnet eyes, but he could see now that she was a compact package, not nearly as long and lanky as he'd first thought. She'd also committed a serious crime against mankind by scraping her hair back into a tight little knot at the base of her neck. No wonder he hadn't noticed the true color. He itched to release that knot and run his fingers through the silken mass. To feel the texture and see the vivid color fanned across her pale shoulders.

Years of hard ranch work had honed her body into lean, tempered strength and contributed to the appealing curve of her legs and backside. She'd also been blessed with ideal-sized breasts, neither too small nor too large, but the sort that filled a man's palms to perfection. When it came to her face, though, nature had gifted her with true beauty.

She had the type of bone structure that would accentuate her loveliness even at ninety, with the pale, creamy complexion of a true redhead. The winged eyebrows, soaring cheekbones and full lush mouth, would have made her features too flawless for his taste if it weren't for the redeeming crook in her otherwise straight nose. He almost grinned. Now how had that happened?

The elevator pinged behind her and she whipped around with an exclamation of relief and swept into the car. Joc followed her in, sparking an interesting combination of reactions—alarm, wariness and a feminine awareness that roused an intense, masculine urge to pursue. The door closed and they began their descent.

"I believe you forgot something." He held out her Stetson.

He'd disconcerted her, breaking through the barriers she'd been swift to erect. "Thanks," she murmured. She took the hat from him and crammed it down on her head, hiding every scrap of hair.

"You're welcome." He reached around her and pushed a button that brought the elevator to a smooth halt.

"What are you doing?" He could hear the hint of

trepidation in her voice and the breathless awareness of his proximity. "Why did you stop the elevator?"

"I'd like to make you another offer."

She cut him off with a graceful sweep of her hand. "Please, don't. I've heard your offers and I'm not interested."

"You haven't heard this one."

She jerked her head in his direction and then away again, fixing her stare on the control panel. If he were a betting man, which he was, he'd be willing to wager a cool million that it took every ounce of self-control in her possession to keep from jabbing at the buttons in order to get the elevator moving again. Her hand inched toward the control panel before she dropped her arms to her sides in clear surrender.

"How many ways do I have to say I'm not interested?" she asked with quiet dignity. "I wasn't interested in any of your previous offers. I won't be interested in this one, either."

"I thought I'd give you the chance to convince me of your disinterest over dinner."

That caught her attention and she turned to confront him. "Dinner?"

"Right. That's the meal that comes after lunch and before bedtime."

Instead of laughing, a hint of a frown crept across her brow. "Why would you want to take me to dinner? You know I'm not going to agree to any offer you might make."

He flicked his thumb against the brim of her hat. It knocked the battered felt toward the back of her head and gave him an unobstructed view of her face. So much character, he marveled. So much strength and determination. And the passion. She smoldered with it, thickening the air with ripe feminine power. What would it be like to ignite all that? To kindle those banked flames into a raging wildfire? He wanted to find out. Needed to. But, first things first.

"How do you know I won't be persuaded to change my mind about buying your ranch? Think about it. You'll have all evening to argue with me. Uninterrupted time where you'll have my full attention. Hours in which you can explain why I should just go away and leave you alone."

"Tempting." She studied him and he saw a wild animal's wariness in her gaze. "What's the catch?"

"What makes you think there's a catch?" he countered.

"Because you're Joc Arnaud and you want something from me."

Smart woman. "You'll have to figure that out for yourself."

"And if it's something I can't give?"

"You say no." He gave her a verbal shove. "You do know the word, don't you?"

She surprised him by absorbing his comment with equanimity, confining herself to a single comeback. "Be careful or you'll find out how well I know it." She took a minute to consider. "Dinner and talk. That's it?"

"That's it."

Unless more happened. Because this wasn't just about business, anymore. There was more between them, something elemental running beneath the surface. It was that something that had Joc coming to an instant decision. Her ranch was of secondary concern, mainly because he'd have that before long, whether she acquiesced to his demands or he wrestled it away with her fighting him over every inch of land. Right now other needs were of far greater urgency. No matter what, he'd have this woman in his bed. Have her until he was sated, regardless of how short or long the taking…or how much she resisted.

"Okay, I agree," she said at last.

"I thought you might," he murmured. He reached around her and released the elevator, allowing it to continue its downward plummet.

No doubt it was taking them both straight to hell.

Rosalyn stared at the elevator doors and fought to regain her self-control. Joc had knocked her Stetson to the back of her head and now she crushed it low on her brow. Okay, so she was hiding her expression from him. So, what? That didn't matter anywhere near as much as the fact that he had her acting like a total idiot. A rock dumb, bat blind, total idiot.

Arnaud had already warned her that he always won. This give and take between them was nothing more than a game to him, an avenue toward another check in the win column of his playbook. For her, the stakes were far higher. Her ranch was her life, keeping its legacy safe for future Oakleys her sole ambition. She'd promised to do just that, a deathbed vow that left no maneuvering room for negotiation or personal preferences.

Granted, Arnaud didn't care about her reasons for

resisting his business proposition. Still… What if she could explain that sort of emotion to him in language he could understand? What if she could talk him into going away and leaving her alone? It wouldn't solve all her problems, but it would solve her most immediate one.

She spared him a swift glance from beneath her lashes. He was staring at her, his lazy grin warning he knew what she'd been thinking. Not that it mattered what counteragenda he might be working on the sly. She'd committed herself to going out to dinner with him and she would. She'd even try to change his mind about buying her out, though she doubted she'd succeed.

Nevertheless, he was right about one thing: spending a little time with him would give her a better handle on his strategy and what her chances were of winning—though at a guess that would be somewhere in the neighborhood of zero to none. She weighed that against the feminine intuition that warned that he wanted far more from her than her property. It filled her with the urge to change her mind and run home to safety, the protective instinct for flight eclipsing the desire to fight. She opened her mouth to give instinct a voice.

"You can't." His voice came from just behind and above.

How had he gotten so close without her noticing? "I can't what?"

"You agreed to dinner and you can't change your mind."

"How did you know—" She closed her mouth with a snap and glared at the elevator doors. "Okay, I get it now."

"Get what?" Laughter. Arnaud was laughing at her!

"I understand why you're so successful. You can read minds."

"Only when the thoughts are strong. Or the emotions," he added.

She winced. Was that his subtle way of telling her he'd picked up on her reaction to him? She needed to get off the ranch more. Date. Get a better grip on the male psyche and how to handle men like Arnaud. Because Mr. Big Bad had quite the grip on the female end of things, which put her at a distinct disadvantage.

"I promised I'd go to dinner with you, and I will." If she sounded reluctant, that couldn't be helped. He'd boxed her in and she didn't like it. "When I give my word, I stick to it."

"As do I."

She turned and studied his expression. Not that it helped much. He had "inscrutable" down to a science. "You'll give me a fair shot at changing your mind?" she asked.

"Yes."

She wanted to pin him down further but didn't have a clue how to do it. They were so mismatched, it was downright pathetic. Still, she'd try her best. What other choice did she have? "Are you open to changing your mind?"

"In my business it pays to be flexible." His expression hardened. "It also pays to go after what you want with every strength, skill and asset at your disposal."

"Thanks for the suggestion. I'll do just that." An idea occurred to her, one that might put her in a better bargaining position. "And I'd like to start by adding an addendum to our agreement."

He lifted an eyebrow. "A negotiation?" he asked, intrigued. "My favorite pastime. What's your addendum?"

"You come to my place for dinner."

He nodded in complete understanding. "You want to negotiate on your own turf. Good move."

He leaned in and it took all her concentration just to inhale and exhale in a normal fashion. His deep-set eyes were the most intense she'd ever seen, the black so absolute she couldn't tell pupil from iris. But it was his mouth that drew her, that stirred something she hadn't felt in years. For such a hard man, his mouth was broad and full and sensual and she couldn't help but wonder what those incredible lips could do to her. Her own lips softened in anticipation. How would it feel to sink into them, to lose herself in their heat? Did he kiss as well as he made money? Chances were excellent he did, which made her all the more curious to find out.

"My turf or yours, it doesn't matter," he was saying. "I don't play softball, Red. My pitch is low, fast and inside. If you don't watch out, it'll put you in the dirt."

It took her a moment to register his comment. Once she did, she took a hasty step away from him. What was wrong with her? She'd been daydreaming about kissing the man, while he'd been figuring out how to steal her land out from under her. "Why are you telling me this?"

"Because you're out of your league."

She didn't know whether to feel outraged or apprehensive. "You're offering me pity advice?"

"Stow your pride and take it," he suggested. "It's the only help you're going to get. From now on, you're on your own."

No question about that. But maybe, just maybe, by having him on her home turf it would give her just enough of an advantage to uncover his weakness. A tantalizing thought occurred, one that opened all sorts of fascinating possibilities.

What if his weakness was *her?*

Two

Normally, Joc would have used his car and driver for the trip to Longhorn Ranch so he could utilize the time to work. On this occasion, he refrained. Somehow, he didn't think showing up in a limousine would go over well, so he drove himself, arriving at the ranch precisely on time.

He was greeted at the door by an elderly woman who wore a sour expression he'd lay odds she'd spent most of her life cultivating. She gave him the once-over before reluctantly admitting him. "You must be Arnaud."

He offered his hand. "Joc Arnaud."

She gave him a firm handshake in return. "Rosalyn's in the kitchen putting the final touches on your meal. She should have been working on bookkeeping. But since she invited you, she felt obligated to do the cooking. I'm Claire, by the way, the Oakley housekeeper."

He gave her the wine he'd brought. "My contribution to dinner."

She eyed it with suspicion. "This the kind that needs to breathe?"

"After nearly twenty years of being corked, I'm sure it'll be grateful for the opportunity," he answered gravely.

She gave a snort of laughter. "Come on, then. I'll show you the way."

He looked around with interest as she escorted him to the back of the ranch house. It was a beautiful place, with polished wooden floors, beamed ceilings and generously sized rooms in an open floor plan. The kitchen proved equally impressive, with a brick hearth and cast-iron stove from a different era mingling with modern-day appliances. Rosalyn stood at a butcher block chopping vegetables with practiced ease.

"I'll finish up here," Claire said in a tone that clearly stated that this was her domain and she wanted all invaders out of it. "Dinner will be ready in thirty minutes."

Rosalyn shot Joc a look of amusement before crossing to the sink and washing her hands. "Thanks, Claire. I appreciate your help."

"I gather she doesn't like feeding the enemy?" Joc inquired as soon as they were out of earshot.

"Mostly she just doesn't like people in her kitchen." Rosalyn opened the door to a snug parlor, complete with a love seat in front of a hickory-scented fire and decanters of liquor arranged on a silver tray. "But she also considers this meeting a mistake."

"She could be right."

In more ways than one. When Rosalyn had first approached him, they'd been in an office setting, both wearing work attire, even if hers had been a battered Stetson, faded jeans, scarred boots and a flannel shirt. But here, in a more intimate setting, the barriers between them had slipped, blurring the line between business and pleasure.

This go-round, she wore her hair loose, the rich waterfall sweeping past her shoulders in a cape of auburn silk. She'd traded in her ranch gear for tawny slacks and a simple ivory blouse, while a plain gold necklace drew attention to the pale length of her throat and the hint of cleavage that peeked from the shadows of her neckline. A touch of makeup emphasized the startling shade of her violet-blue eyes and made her lips appear fuller and softer. Kissable.

She lifted an eyebrow. "If you think this is a mistake, then why did you suggest dinner in the first place?"

He fought his way back to reality, struggling to regain his focus. He was here on business. That he had to remind himself of that fact didn't bode well for the rest of the evening. "I hoped we could come to an agreement in a more relaxed setting."

"Speaking of which…" She gestured toward the sideboard. "Would you like a drink?"

"Single malt, if you have it."

"Oh, we have it."

Something in her tone snagged his attention. "You don't care for whiskey?"

"On the contrary." She poured them both a drink and joined him by the fire, handing him one of the glasses. "I indulge on rare occasions."

They sat next to each other on the love seat. To his amusement Rosalyn buried her hip against one end of the narrow couch in an attempt to keep as much distance between them as possible. "What occasions do you feel warrant a drink?" he asked, genuinely interested.

"Anniversaries." She flinched from some memory, and the firelight flickered across the elegant planes of her face, revealing a heartbreaking vulnerability. "And when I'm working on the ranch accounts."

What anniversaries? Judging by her drawn expression they weren't celebratory ones. He'd have to recheck her dossier and dig into her past a bit more in order to discover what had caused such a deep hurt. He deliberately kept his response light. "I assume bookkeeping isn't your favorite task?"

"As far as I'm concerned, it requires serious fortification." Her gaze grew pointed. "Sort of like when dealing with you."

"I know a few people like that."

"There are actually people out there who drive you to drink, Arnaud?" His comment had distracted her and some of the pain and tension ebbed. She also relaxed into the cushions so they almost touched. "Sounds like my kind."

"It's my sister. And she is your kind."

"MacKenzie?"

He shook his head. "MacKenzie is my half sister. Same father, different mothers. She drives me to drink, but for different reasons. And I sure as hell wouldn't waste a good single malt on her. No, I'm talking about my full sister, Ana, as well as her husband." He sipped his whiskey. "Or should I say His Highness, Prince Lander Montgomery of Verdonia."

Rosalyn buried her nose in the glass. "Not my kind, after all."

He stretched his legs out toward the fire and smiled. His sister was also a fiery redhead, while his brother-in-law was one of the most protective and honorable men Joc had ever met. Lander had initially become engaged to his sister in an attempt to protect her reputation. He'd even given up a shot at the throne of Verdonia for the good of the country.

"They're both very much your kind. Direct. Down-to-earth. Protective. And they both enjoy flaying a strip or two off my hide whenever the mood takes them. We've had some interesting run-ins."

"Huh. I'd have said your hide was too tough to flay." She swiveled to inspect him, causing a strand of hair to drift across her face. She gave him a swift, searching glance that made him want to pull her into his arms and discover if she tasted as good as she looked. "Maybe I should call them for suggestions."

"I think you're managing just fine on your own."

The strands of hair continued to cling to her face and he reached out without conscious design, intent only on brushing it aside. It was a simple contact, the tips of his fingers barely grazing the fine-boned curve of her cheek in order to sweep the spill of hair away from her eyes. And yet, his instantaneous reaction caught him off guard. Heat poured through him, as though he'd fallen headlong into the popping flames just a few feet away. The slight hitch in Rosalyn's breath told him he wasn't the only one affected. She stared at him, her eyes startled. He'd thrown her. Badly. He felt it rippling through her and saw it reflected in the tautness of her features. Her eyes darkened to a shade of blue the sky took on somewhere between dusk and nightfall. And her mouth—that plump, ripe mouth—trembled in a way that tempted him almost beyond endurance and made him want to kiss away her apprehension.

One touch. It had been one casual, thoughtless touch, a touch that never would have happened if it hadn't been for that rich red hair and those glorious eyes. But the instant he'd run his fingers across her creamy skin, he'd lost it. If they'd been anywhere else, he'd have tumbled her to the floor and taken her, and to hell with the consequences.

What was it about the woman that reduced him to his most basic and primitive instincts? He was a man who prided himself on his self-control, who used that control, along with his innate intelligence and ability to see the big picture and get what he wanted. How was it possible to lose all that with a single touch? It had never happened before, not once in all his thirty-four years, nor with a single one of the women he'd taken to his bed.

He tossed back the last of his whiskey before shooting her a hard look. "We're in trouble. You realize that, don't you?"

Rosalyn shuddered. With that one single touch, wanton desire spilled across her skin in a wave as hot and humid and gripping as Dallas in August. With the heat came the sizzle, a buzz of sensation that went from her cheek straight to the pit of her stomach. She was barely aware of what he said after releasing her. Damn it! She was in deep trouble.

She shot to her feet to give herself some breathing room. Her hand tightened around her glass and she tossed back her whiskey in a single, disjointed movement before returning his look with a hard one of her own. "That can't happen again."

"How are you going to stop it?" he asked, genuinely curious.

"Distance would be a good start."

Her frankness made him smile. He stood as well, throwing a question over his shoulder as he returned his glass to the sideboard. "Is it any better now that I'm across the room?"

"Yes." She thrust a hand through her hair. "No."

"I agree."

She regarded him warily. "So what do we do now?"

A knock sounded at the door and Claire's voice boomed through the heavy wood. "Dinner's on. Shake a leg in there."

Joc crossed the room until they stood toe to toe. Somehow she managed to stand there without giving away the wash of emotions cascading through her. But she couldn't hide the truth from herself, no matter how hard she tried. She wanted him to touch her again, wanted it with a passion that almost had her quivering.

"I suggest we eat," he said in reply to a question she'd already forgotten. "What happens after that is up to you."

"Nothing is going to happen," she stated without

hesitation. "Nothing other than you climbing into your fancy car and returning to Dallas."

"Then neither of us has anything to worry about." He inclined his head toward the door. "Shall we go?"

She hesitated, anxious to recover some of the ground she'd lost and remind them both of why she'd agreed to dine with him. "You promised that I'd have your full and undivided attention. That you'd give me a fair shot at changing your mind about buying my ranch."

"I gave you my word and I'll keep it."

She'd have to be satisfied with that. Together they crossed to the dining room. With every step Rosalyn ran through her game plan. She was a cards-on-the-table type of woman, and she didn't intend to change that with Arnaud. So she'd be blunt with him about why she refused to sell out. But she'd also attempt to unearth any weakness he might possess and exploit it. After all, she wasn't a total fool, not when it came to the safety and security of her ranch. So far, the only weakness she'd discovered involved her and a bed. And as much as that appealed, she'd be an idiot to use it. With her luck he'd walk away with everything she held most dear. No, she needed to spend the next hour or two getting a better handle on him and how she might win this war that had erupted between them.

"Nice," he complimented as they entered the dining room.

Despite his comment, she couldn't help but see her home through his eyes and the sight left her flinching. This was a man accustomed to the best life had to offer, a man worth billions. How plain and countrified her home must appear to him, with its simple wood table decorated with her grandmother's best linen and her great-grandmother's rose-patterned china. Rosalyn had even had the unmitigated nerve to think her meal of pot roast and home-grown vegetables would appeal to a palate fine-tuned to five-star gourmet cuisine.

"It's not fancy."

He must have caught the defensive edge in her voice, and he turned to face her. "Are you apologizing for your lifestyle? Because if you don't like it, I can fix that for you."

It was precisely what she'd been doing and the knowledge hit hard. Her hands balled into fists. She had nothing to apologize for. Absolutely nothing. "No, thanks. I like what I have."

He offered the smile that never failed to sink into her bones and slip through her veins like quicksilver. "I thought I had you for a minute there."

"Not a chance."

They took a seat at the dining room table, she at the head, he on her right. She left him to eat his first course in peace—the salad she'd been preparing when he'd arrived. Most of the vegetables were ones growing just outside the kitchen door, where similar household crops had been tended and cultivated by the women of the house for as long as the homestead had stood.

It wasn't until they'd finished their main course that he turned their conversation to business. "Shall we negotiate our differences or would you rather table it for the evening?" he asked.

"Since this is my only opportunity to change your mind, I think we'll negotiate." She shoved her plate to one side. "Let's start with something easy. Why do you want my ranch?"

"It sits at the heart of land I own," he answered promptly.

"Land you purchased within the last year."

"It only became available this past year." He lifted an eyebrow. "Does it matter when I purchased the property?"

She shook her head. "No. What matters is that you've wasted your time and money since there's no chance of acquiring my ranch."

To her frustration, he simply shrugged. "Time will tell."

Claire appeared with their dessert and Rosalyn stewed over his calm certainty that she'd ever consider selling her home. Unable to stand it another minute, she said, "Explain it to me, Arnaud. Why are you buying up this particular section of Texas? What could you possibly want with it when you could have any other place in the world for the asking?" Her hair drifted into her face again, and she swept it behind one ear, aware that he followed the movement with far too much interest. "Is it the history attached to my place? Is that it? Are you after roots? A heritage? What?"

She asked the exact wrong series of questions. His expression closed over into a sterner mask than she'd ever seen before. "Why would I want those?"

"Don't play ignorant with me." She fought to contain her anger with only limited success. "You know what I'm asking. For you, this land is a possession. You want, therefore you take. For me, it's something far more personal." She leaned forward, her voice ripe with passion. "It's a part of me. A part of my heritage. A part of who I am and where I come from."

He gave her a hard, unwavering look. "That's a lie handed down through generations of Oakleys. You are not the land. You live on it for a brief period in the grand scheme of things. A hundred years from now, two hundred, what happens here tonight won't matter. No one will even remember it. We will have come and gone. Only the land will remain." He paused long enough for that to sink in before summing it up with characteristic succinctness. "It's dirt, Red. Nothing more than acres of dirt."

"You can't honestly believe that?"

"I promised I'd tell you the truth and I am." He opened a door she suspected he kept shut tight in the normal course of things. "I assume you know I'm illegitimate, so I suppose it's only natural you'd think I want your ranch because of the history behind it, or the roots or heritage it represents."

She allowed her doubt to show. "Are you sure that's not it?"

"Not even a little. How long has your family owned this land? A hundred years? Two hundred? If I wanted roots and heritage I could have gone to Europe and married into lineages far more impressive than what anyone in the States can claim. It wouldn't have been difficult. When I was visiting my sister in Verdonia, there were plenty of opportunities. Family that stretched back close to a millennium. Estates that could have given me a title and roots and prestige, if that's what I wanted." He spoke with a stunning disdain, his comment edged with a bitter chill. "I don't."

"You must recognize that it's important to others,"

she argued. "You bought your own family's homestead. I heard you discussing it with MacKenzie. Keeping the Hollister land intact must have some meaning for you to have purchased it and now refuse to sell."

"I haven't stepped foot on that land, and I never will."

Shock held her silent for a long moment. "You don't want it for yourself, but you also won't allow the Hollisters to buy it back?"

"I have my reasons." Something in his eyes warned that she'd opened a door that should have remained locked. "I recognize that some people allow the ownership of property to define who they are. But it's an illusion. You're the last of the Oakley line, Red. When you marry and have children, they won't be Oakleys. They won't bear the Oakley name. And what if you sold the ranch…or lost it? Does living on Oakley land define who you are? Are you no longer that person when you leave it?"

She swept the question aside. "It's my land," she retorted. "You can't force me to give that up or to sell it if I don't want to."

"True. But at some point I'll hit on something you want more than your land, just like Meredith Hollister. And that's when you'll sell."

"I won't." She made the words as adamant and uncompromising as possible. "It was shortsighted of you to buy the surrounding property without knowing for certain whether or not I'd sell. That's just plain bad business—a first in the career of the great Joc Arnaud."

He surprised her by inclining his head in acknowledgment. "The land around yours suddenly became available and I had to act fast. I was told you were not only willing to sell, but eager, or I wouldn't have gone through with the deal."

Understanding dawned. "Those two employees of yours, the two who've been after me this past year... They lied to you?" She shook her head. "That was brave of them."

She shivered at the darkness that settled over his expression and turned his eyes to black agates. "More stupid than brave. And my *former* employees won't be troubling you anymore. I've taken over the job of persuading you to sell, personally."

Heaven help her. "Just out of curiosity, if I did sell Longhorn to you, what would you put here in place of my ranch?"

He hesitated, refreshing their wineglasses, before responding. "This isn't for public consumption, yet, but it's only fair you know. I'm building a complex for the various Arnaud corporations and business interests."

She stared in dismay. "What sort of complex?"

"A huge one," he admitted. "In addition to the actual office buildings, there will also be day-care centers, spas, medical facilities, gyms, a sports complex, cafeterias. Even a movie theater or two. I also plan to build apartments and condos for employees who want to live within walking distance of their job."

Stunned, she grabbed her wineglass and took a long sip of the rich, floral-scented pinot noir. It sounded like he intended to build a miniature city. She'd read about computer companies and Internet corporations doing something similar, and been impressed by the breadth and scope of their endeavor. But those were built at a safe distance, not in her own backyard. Hell, not *on* her backyard. A slight tremor betrayed her alarm and she carefully returned her wineglass to the table.

"That's quite an undertaking." And must have been under consideration for years, she realized in dismay. If so, she'd have an impossible time changing his mind. "No wonder you need your own corner of Texas."

"And why I'll do anything to get it." He leaned back in his chair, his expression relaxing into a smile that never failed to distract her. "Now that you know what I plan to do and how committed I am to purchasing your property, you're in a unique position. Not many can claim that when it comes to negotiating with me. Name your price. Any price you want, Red, and I'll pay it."

"You still don't get it, do you?" She gestured toward his plate. "Are you finished eating?" At his nod, she shoved back from the table. "Come with me. I want to show you something."

She escaped the table and promptly caught her boot heel in the loose hallway runner just outside the dining room. If Joc hadn't caught her at the last second, she'd have taken a nasty fall down the stone steps leading to the sunken living room.

"Are you okay?" he asked.

They were touching again, something she'd sworn wouldn't happen. She felt the tension vibrating through him, a mirror image of her own. "I keep meaning to have one of the boys tack that down," she replied in a breathless voice. "But I keep forgetting."

"I suggest you move it up on your priority list. Next time I might not be here to catch you."

Her mouth curved into a reluctant smile. "Actually…that's the whole idea. I'm trying to get rid of you, remember?"

Pulling free of his grasp, she led the way outside to where her Jeep stood parked beneath an overhang attached to the barn. She made a beeline for it. He followed, climbing into the passenger seat while she hopped behind the wheel and cranked over the ignition.

The engine started with a roar and she wrestled the gearshift into reverse. It was a cantankerous old vehicle, but she had a fondness for it because it was the first car she'd ever driven. It could also access almost every part of Longhorn Ranch. She eased off the clutch and the Jeep bucked with all the affront of a saddle-shy bronco. Then it stalled, quivering beneath the fading sunlight. Refiring the engine, she fishtailed through the mud from the previous night's deluge before the wheels found purchase. The instant they did, she punched the gas.

She took the rut-filled path deeper into Oakley land, between pastures filled with cattle, one of them showcasing the longhorn for which the ranch had been named. She guided the Jeep toward the old homestead, to where it had all begun, in the hopes that seeing it would provide a more eloquent explanation of what this land meant to her, and succeed where mere words had failed. She downshifted as she tackled the final rise leading to the heart of her property. The storm had turned the dirt road into a sea of mud and she fought to keep the vehicle from bogging down. The path curved sharply and she hit the muddy bend in a flat-out skid.

The Jeep let out a gasp of relief at having made the steep grade and died not far from an ancient single-room cabin. Rosalyn sat silently for a moment, allowing Joc to look his fill. "It's the original Oakley homestead. My ancestors constructed it from riverrock."

He shook his head. "Can you imagine starting your life in this wilderness, with only those four walls protecting you from the elements?" He glanced at her, allowing his admiration to show. "Brave people."

"That's what I come from, Joc. People who carved a home from nothing. Who faced not only the elements, but dealt with all the war and strife the past couple hundred years have thrown at them."

The fading sun painted the stones in deceptively gentle shades of pink and mauve, and even managed to make the picket fence delineating the weed-choked yard appear whimsical rather than ramshackle. She exited the Jeep and circled the cabin. Joc followed silently as she led him to a small cemetery not far from the original homestead.

Close to two hundred years of Oakleys were tucked beneath the protective embrace of a towering stand of cottonwoods. He took his time wandering among the gravestones. The most poignant were the ones he approached last, the recent ones. Five sites were huddled close together. Four of them—Rosalyn's grandfather, her parents and a five-year-old brother—had died a full decade ago, all on the same day. The other, her grandmother, just a year ago.

"The anniversaries," he murmured somberly. "These are the anniversaries you toast with a glass of whiskey."

"Yes."

"What happened to them?"

She crouched beside the gravesites, clearing them of the few weeds that had cropped up since her last visit a few days before. "Small-plane crash my senior year in high school."

"And you?" She couldn't detect a single scrap of emotion in the question, and yet she could feel it. It crashed outward from him in waves of concern, a concern that took her by surprise. "Were you onboard?"

"No. I was sick that day. Nanna stayed home with me. Otherwise…" She shrugged. "We wouldn't be in our current predicament. The ranch would have been sold long ago."

"God, Red. I'm so sorry. And I thought my formative years were bad."

She rocked back on her heels and gazed up at him. "You need to understand something, Joc. When my family died, I lost a huge part of myself. All I had left to fill that hole was this ranch and my grandmother. I quickly realized that I could give up or carry on."

"You carried on."

She nodded and swept a hand in a wide arc. "All this you see around me? It's my legacy. My responsibility. It's as much a part of me as my blood and bones. It's part of my flesh. Part of who and what I am. I promised my grandmother on her deathbed that I'd do everything within my power to protect that legacy, and I will." She stood, rubbing the bits of grass and dirt from her hands. "You want my land, Joc. Well, I'm part and parcel of this land. You can't separate me from it or pull my roots loose any more than you can break the connection that joins me to every single soul in this cemetery. I won't sell, and that's final."

The sun hovered on the horizon, a burning ball of red, throwing its dying rays outward in a final blazing explosion. Joc stood within its burning embrace, sculpted in harsh contours of light and shadow, the embodiment of his Native American ancestry. A determined expression settled over his face, one that left her shivering.

"I guess there's nothing left to discuss," he limited himself to saying.

"Then you'll leave me alone?"

He simply stared at her for a long, silent moment. "You're asking too much. I won't leave you alone. I can't."

"How can you think I'll ever sell? How can you believe for even one minute—"

"I'm not talking about your ranch. It's you I can't leave alone."

He came for her then, eating up the ground in a half dozen long strides. The instant he reached her, he caught her in his arms. "Don't fight me. Not on this front." And then he consumed her.

She'd always found a first kiss to be tentative. A slow sampling, oftentimes awkward, as lips fought to discover the right angle and pressure. But with Joc that awkwardness didn't exist. His kiss was everything she'd anticipated and then some. Their lips mated with an ease and certainty that should have taken dozens of kisses to achieve.

Everything about him epitomized power and strength, and she found that true of his kiss, as well. He combined those qualities with a ruthless demand that stunned both body and mind. His mouth slid across hers in blatant hunger, stifling any thought of protest. She hesitated, aware that she should pull away, but wanting just another second or two of this incredible bliss. In that moment of indecision, he slid his hand down the length of her spine to the hollow just above her backside and urged her closer, locking her in place between his thighs.

Their bodies melded, the fit sheer perfection. He had a hard, muscular frame, lean and well-sculpted. It surprised her since it seemed more suited to a fellow rancher than a man who made his living behind a desk. Unable to resist, she measured the breadth of his shoulders, shocked to discover her fingers trembled. He did that to her, coaxing to the surface emotions she wanted to deny, but couldn't.

He cupped her face and teased the corners of her mouth with his thumbs until her lips parted. The instant she relaxed, he deepened the kiss, dipping inward. She should fight her way free of their embrace, and put an end to this farce. But she didn't want to. To her eternal shame, she kissed him back, allowing him to forge a connection between them that wouldn't easily be severed, regardless of her preference in the matter.

She needed this moment, needed tonight. If she were honest, she'd admit that she secretly yearned for Joc's possession. But a tiny rational part of her clung to reason and shouted a warning about all she stood to lose if she gave herself to this man. The price would prove high if she weren't careful, destroying everything she'd worked so hard to build.

Even knowing that, she couldn't bring herself to put an end to their embrace. It wasn't until she heard the small growl of triumph that rumbled through his chest that she came to her senses. With an exclamation of horror, she yanked free of his arms and retreated several stumbling steps. She touched her mouth with fingers that shook, stunned by how he'd managed to turn her world from reason to insanity with a single kiss.

"Tell me how we're supposed to go our separate ways now," he demanded.

"I can't… I won't—" She shook her head. "You're not going to romance my ranch out from under me."

"This has nothing to do with your ranch," he insisted impatiently. "This is strictly between the two of us."

"There is no *us*. This is nothing more than—" She broke off, hoping the gathering shadows hid her discomfort.

"Sex?" he offered with a humorous smile.

"Fine. Yes. It's nothing more than sex. And I won't let you use it to take my ranch."

He laughed, the sound dark and dangerous, penetrating deep inside her. "You don't get it, Red. I've changed my mind." Two swift steps had him within touching range again. "It isn't just your ranch I want anymore."

He stroked her cheek, just as he had before dinner. And she reacted every bit as strongly, swaying helplessly toward him, before locking her knees in place and resisting with every ounce of determination she possessed.

She knew. On some deep, purely feminine level, she knew the answer before she even asked the question. "What do you want now?"

"You."

Three

"Forget it. My ranch isn't for sale, no matter what you offer." Naked passion shot through Rosalyn's words and was reflected in her face. "And neither am I."

"I know you're not for sale, and I'd never insult you by suggesting such a thing. But you want me every bit as much as I want you. Deny it, if it makes you feel better. Fight if you want. But in the end neither of us is going to be able to resist." Joc stepped back, giving her some much needed breathing space. "I have a suggestion, one that might take care of our little problem."

"You're going away and leaving me alone?"

He didn't take the hint. "Too late, Red. You walked through my door of your own volition. Don't blame me if I refuse to let you go."

"I can say no." She shook her head, as though to clear it. "I will say no."

He couldn't help smiling at her confusion. "I hope to God you do. It would make things easier." Then he grew serious. "One night, Red. One night together and we should be able to satisfy whatever this is between us."

Her eyes widened in disbelief. "What are you talking about?"

"I'm taking a short trip tomorrow. Come with me. No ranch talk. No negotiating. No contention. Just you and me and a single night of romance."

Her breath caught before escaping in a rush. "You can't be serious."

He offered a fleeting smile. "Well...if you insist on negotiating the sale of your ranch, I won't refuse. But I'd rather focus on pleasure and save business for some other time. What do you say?"

"That this is insane."

His smile grew at her bluntness. "Granted. But so what? Let's be insane together. Come with me, Rosalyn. You won't regret it, I promise."

She was tempted, so very tempted. She forced herself to take another step backward, when what she wanted more than anything was to throw herself into his arms and surrender to madness. *She was his weakness,* she realized, the earlier suspicion easing toward fact. But it didn't bring her any satisfaction since she refused to use that to gain an advantage. If she were so foolish as to take him up on his offer, she'd do it because she wanted to be in his bed and not for any other reason.

"I can't." She forced herself to be honest. "I won't."

"You've never done a one-night stand before, have you?"

"No." She couldn't help laughing. "Nor do I think it would be wise to start with you."

He tilted his head to one side, his eyes shrewd and watchful. "Is there anything I can say or do that might change your mind? Drop my attempt to buy your ranch, for instance?"

Her humor faded. "Not cool, Arnaud. I don't handle business that way and I never will."

He appeared pleased by her answer. "I was hoping you'd say that."

She didn't like the direction he'd taken the discussion. Time to put an end to it. "It's getting dark. We should go."

Spinning on her heel, she headed back to her Jeep, not caring if Joc followed or not. He arrived at the driver-side door at the same instant she did and reached around her to open it. His voice slid through the gathering dusk, low and filled with regret.

"I've offended you and I'm sorry. I'm accustomed to a world where people have agendas, most of which are hidden. I can't trust what I see on the surface. I have to constantly look beneath in order to discover their true motives."

"I'm not like that," she retorted without turning around. "What you see is what you get."

"I don't trust easily."

This time she did turn, practically finding herself in his arms. "You're wrong, Joc. It's not that you don't trust easily. You don't trust at all."

"Maybe I could with you."

She shook her head. "I doubt it. You'd always wonder if our relationship wasn't my way of protecting my ranch. You'd always suspect everything I said or did because of Longhorn. That's why you're offering a one-night stand. You're hoping we'll get each other out of our systems, so that we can put our relationship back on a business footing."

He gazed down at her, impressed. "Honey, you're wasted on a ranch. You should come work for me."

"No, thanks." Retreating, she slid behind the steering wheel. "Let's go, Arnaud. We've had our fun. It's time to be enemies again."

They returned to the ranch in silence and she parked the Jeep in its space beside the barn. One of her hands, Duff, approached as they crossed the yard toward Joc's vehicle. "Excuse me, Miss Rosalyn. I'll be heading into town tomorrow on a mail run and wondered if you had anything you needed me to do while I was there."

"I have a list. I'll also be doing accounts tonight so if you'd stop by the house first thing in the morning, you can pick up the list, as well as the bills and get them posted. And make sure that mortgage payment is the first one into the mailbox."

"Sure thing." He tipped his hat to both of them and then headed for the bunkhouse.

"I gather from your expression there's another glass of single malt in your immediate future," Joc said once Duff was out of earshot.

"It's entirely possible. The spring calving has put me seriously behind on everything except getting the bills paid." She grimaced. "I can't remember the last time I balanced my accounts."

"Take it from someone who knows... That's not a good idea."

"Thanks for the tip."

He smiled at the reluctant concession. "And thank you for dinner. If you change your mind about tomorrow, I'll send a car for you at eight sharp."

"Tempting, but I'll pass."

He started to reach for her, but after sparing a swift glance in the direction of the bunkhouse, changed his mind. "You don't need to bring anything with you. Just come. I'll take care of all the rest. You've worked hard all your life, Rosalyn. Let me give you one night of pleasure."

Almost. She almost caved, but subdued the helpless agreement at the last possible instant. "Please go."

He lowered his head until his mouth practically brushed hers. "Please come." The words blew across her lips like a warm, tropical breeze, filled with exotic scents and tastes.

She'd like to, more than anything. But she didn't dare say it aloud.

He read her mind, anyway. "Do it. My car's going to show up here at eight tomorrow no matter what you say right now. But if you decide to join me, I promise you won't regret it. We'll spend a night together that neither of us will forget."

And then he was gone, leaving her standing there in the gathering darkness, dreaming of what it would be like to share a single night of incredible bliss with Joc Arnaud.

* * *

Promptly at eight the next morning Rosalyn found herself climbing into the back of Joc's limo onto butter-soft leather seats. All the while she called herself every type of fool. After the intensity of the harsh morning sunlight, the interior seemed dim and cool, probably because the windows were darkened for privacy and the AC ran at full-blast. It was also quiet. Too quiet. And rich. If money had a special blended perfume, this place would reek of it.

Why was she doing this? Clearly she'd lost her mind. During the forty minutes it took to rendezvous with Joc, she forced herself to sit without fidgeting, deliberately holding the full weight of her foolishness at bay by keeping her mind a blank.

"First time?" Joc asked the minute he joined her.

She jumped. "What? Oh, in a limo? Yes."

"I didn't expect you to come." He tilted his head to one side. "How long did that decision take?"

"From the time you left right up until I found myself walking out to your limo and getting in." Before then she'd had every intention of sending the car on its way. Now all she could do was silently curse her impulsive stupidity. She stared at Joc in a combination of dawning horror and disbelief. "I just told Claire goodbye and that I'd see her tomorrow and to hold down the fort while I was gone."

He chuckled in genuine amusement. "I gather you left before she had time to bar the doors and tie you to the nearest chair."

"Pretty much."

"And now you're having second thoughts."

"Was it the shaking that gave it away, or the hyper-ventilating?"

"Don't worry. I'll be gentle."

"I think that's what the Big Bad Wolf said right before he ate Little Red Riding Hood," she muttered in reply.

That won her another laugh. He leaned forward and removed her hat, tossing it onto the seat across from them. Without the protective shade from the brim, she felt far too exposed and folded her hands in her lap with a grip so tight her knuckles blanched. She frowned at the dichotomy of battered Stetson resting on pristine cream leather.

"Now there's a sight I never thought to see. Not a comfortable fit, is it?"

"You might be surprised at how comfortable the fit becomes, given time." He tilted his head to one side, assessing her reaction to his comment. "I could prove how comfortable it would be, but it might take more than a single night."

Even she could read between those lines. "I'll pass."

Twenty minutes later they arrived at a private airport. The limo was waved onto the tarmac and pulled to a halt not far from a corporate jet. In no time they were up the steps, aboard the plane and buckled into the spacious seats. She stared at Joc, struggling for something innocuous to say, something that had nothing to do with their plans for the next twenty-four hours.

"So, where are we going?" she asked.

He accepted her nervous volley with equanimity. "A small island between the Gulf and the Caribbean called Isla de los Deseos."

The information left her shifting in her seat. "I didn't realize we'd be going so far."

He signaled the flight attendant and held up two fingers. The next instant they were each presented a cup of coffee before their server made herself scarce. "I promised you a romantic evening, and I guarantee it'll be one. This particular jet was built for speed. It'll only take a few hours to reach Deseos. In the meantime, relax. There's a selection of movies you can watch and we have a full library of books and magazines. When's the last time you had a break from work?"

She stared at him without speaking, which was answer enough.

"I gather you don't believe in vacations?" he probed.

"I own a ranch," she replied, as though that single statement said it all. And maybe it did.

"You have employees. Or isn't the word 'delegation' part of your vocabulary."

"It's in there somewhere. I just can't—" She broke off and sipped her coffee.

He knew what she'd been about to say. She couldn't afford to delegate. A wave of protectiveness caught him by surprise. She shouldn't have to work so hard. If he took the ranch off her hands, maybe she wouldn't have to. His mouth twisted at the thought. How altruistic of him.

"Put your chair back and relax. I have an hour or so of work to do before we land."

To his surprise, she did as he suggested. When he next looked up it was to find her fast asleep. Her hair had slipped over one shoulder like a silken flow of lava, just skimming the upper curve of her breast. She'd turned her face toward him at some point and sleep eased the contours, making her appear young and innocent. The upper few snaps of her shirt had come undone and he caught a glimpse of fragile bone structure and the soft curve of rounded flesh before it vanished into the confines of a utilitarian white bra.

He forced his attention back to his work, examining the final details of the partnership he'd be dismantling early the next morning. But through it all he could see that combination of creamy white alongside deep auburn. Could feel the tug and hear the whisper that urged him to wake Red with a kiss.

And he wanted. Wanted with a growing passion that defied all attempts to control and threatened all he hoped to achieve.

Rosalyn woke with a start only moments after they'd landed and Joc watched her struggle to bring her brain online. In those first few moments he suspected she didn't know where she was, whether it was night or day, or how she'd gotten wherever she'd ended up. He knew the feeling well enough to recognize it in her expression. It also allowed him to see her with her guard down, at her most open and vulnerable.

She turned her head and he sat there, watching her with an intensity that warned he found her more interesting than any woman in memory. The instant she caught him staring, her barriers slammed into place, shutting him out of the one place he most wanted to be.

"We just landed on Isla de los Deseos," he said. "We got here by corporate jet. It's one in the afternoon,

Thursday. That's Dallas time, not local. You agreed to spend the night with me, something I'm sure you're now regretting."

She straightened in her seat. "Thanks. That fills in the gaps beautifully." She spoke with a hint of formality, and yet her voice slid through him, warm and deep and sleep-roughened.

"You must have been tired." He stood, though that meant ducking a bit to fit his six-foot-three-inch frame beneath the five-and-a-half-foot ceiling. "You work too hard."

"How would you know?" She waved the question aside. "Never mind. Knowing you, you've had me investigated up one side and down the other."

He didn't bother confirming it, since it was the truth. "Hungry?" he asked.

"Starving."

"Then I'll show you to our room and we'll grab a bite to eat."

She followed him off the plane, exiting into heat and humidity only a little less intense than Dallas, although the quality of the air felt far different here. He wondered if she'd notice. For some reason, the dampness had a lighter, mistier quality to it, a soft stroke across the skin instead of a thick blanket. She took a deep breath and he acknowledged her soft exclamation of delight with a nod of agreement.

"Different, isn't it?"

"Sweet. And…and exotic. Is it the flowers?"

"The flowers. The salt air. The spices. It gets to you after a while. Forces you to relax."

After a short drive from the airport, they arrived at a resort complex. A bellman escorted them directly to a large cabaña tucked off to one side of the main hotel. It rambled across a lush, fern-covered rise with a breathtaking view of the ocean on one side and verdant rain forest on the other. Inside, large airy rooms flowed one into the other. Terra cotta slate composed the entranceway, while the rest of the rooms featured hand-scraped bamboo flooring covered with woven area rugs. All of the rooms had been decorated with refreshing accents in exotic shades of mango, kiwi and pineapple. Overhead, a soft breeze stirred from the wicker ceiling fans. It was a welcoming haven, a place where they both could relax and give in to fantasy.

"I arranged for a picnic lunch. I thought we'd eat it down by the lagoon." He gestured toward one of the main corridors. "You'll find everything you need in the bedroom at the end of the hall. It's stocked with all the basic amenities. There should be a bathing suit that'll fit you. Go ahead and change and we'll head out."

It didn't take her long. Just as he'd finished tossing ice cold bottled water into the lunch basket, she reappeared wearing an emerald-green maillot with a matching floral print wrap tied at her waist. She'd replaced her Stetson with a wide-brimmed straw hat and a pair of oversize sunglasses were perched on the end of her nose. She held a bottle of sunscreen in one hand.

"I managed to get everywhere but my back. Do you mind? I burn like crazy, otherwise."

He suspected she wouldn't appreciate it if he turned

dousing her with lotion into foreplay. And judging by her expression she expected him to do just that. Instead he drizzled the cream onto her back and rubbed it in with brisk efficiency. She relaxed when it became clear that he didn't plan to jump her, which told him he'd elected the perfect tack. Rosalyn might have chosen to come on this little jaunt, but the more rational part of her still dealt with the potential fallout from that decision.

He could tell she wanted him. And that simple fact had thrown her completely off-kilter.

"Is this one of the hotel suites?" she asked as they exited the cabaña and headed for a gorgeous curve of beach.

"Owner's residence."

She shot him a wry smile. "I should have known." She turned her attention toward the water and nodded in approval. "It's stunning."

Pristine-white sand flowed toward a protected lagoon, stumbling over the occasional coconut husk before sliding beneath crystalline aquamarine waves. A row of palms fenced off the area, bravely defending their line to prevent the spill of jungle forest from encroaching onto the powdery sand. To his amusement, a few wayward palms had abandoned their post and congregated halfway between wave and woodland. Most tempting of all, some truly brilliant individual had strung a pair of hammocks between the palms.

Rosalyn appropriated one of them, flipping her hat and sunglasses onto it, along with her wrap. Tossing a quick grin over her shoulder, she made a beeline for the crystalline water and struck out across the lagoon with long, swift strokes. He shook his head in amusement.

He had to hand it to her—the woman worked hard at relaxing, swimming with utter focus and intensity. He joined her, matching his tempo to hers.

Twenty minutes later, she paused in her exertions. "I can't swim another minute. I need food."

"Now that I can provide."

He caught her hand in his and dragged her from the water. Her skin was the pale, milky alabaster of a true redhead and he didn't bother to hide his admiration. "For someone who spends her days out of doors, you have very little tan."

"I inherited my complexion from my mother." She paused at the ocean's edge to wring out her hair before tossing it over her shoulder. It tumbled in a heavy, wet curtain halfway down her back, the sun splintering the deep auburn into shades that ranged from autumn russet to red-gold. "She and my grandmother drummed the importance of good skin care into me practically from the time I was born."

"Savvy women."

A hint of sorrow shadowed her expression. "Yes, they were."

"I'm sorry," he said, instantly contrite. "I wanted today to be romantic, not sad."

"That's okay. I'll survive it." She crossed the sand toward the hammock and flopped onto it with impressive dexterity. Wriggling into a comfortable position, she stretched like a cat. The emerald-green bathing suit pulled taut across boyish hips and decidedly unboyish breasts, the wet material leaving little to the imagination. She was quite simply glorious, her figure sculpted into a lean musculature, no doubt the result of years of intensive ranch work.

"Okay, Arnaud. Feed me before I pass out from hunger."

He flipped open the lunch basket. "I think I have just the perfect thing to satisfy both of our appetites."

All through lunch he kept the conversation light and casual, using the opportunity to study her. She was one of the most beautiful and intriguing women he'd ever met—a temptation he found irresistible. Unfortunately that temptation created something of a dilemma.

He frowned. Time to face facts. There was a ranch war coming, one he hadn't anticipated, granted. But it was a war he intended to win. Not that winning would prove easy or decisive. Nor would it come without a carefully executed plan of action. He allowed himself one last, long minute to study his battleground as she swayed delicately in the breeze, savoring a variety of fruit wedges.

Oh, yeah. There was definitely a war coming. And he knew, without doubt or hesitation, where that final, deciding skirmish would take place.

He and his lovely rancher would pitch that final battle in bed.

The afternoon proved to be one of the best Rosalyn could ever remember. Joc went out of his way to offer her every pleasure—food, drink, amusing company and an ocean of gentle waves and warm caresses.

Eventually she abandoned her hammock in favor of his. Or rather, he forced her to abandon it when he picked her up and tumbled with her into his. They stayed there for an endless time, quietly talking as they watched the sun work its way toward the horizon. As the afternoon waned, the sky took on a palette of colors so breathtaking, it brought tears to her eyes.

It was then that she realized that most of the conversation had revolved around her and how she'd handled the management of her ranch after the death of her parents. She hadn't learned anything about Joc or his background. She settled herself more comfortably into his arms. Time to change all that. "You said you had a traumatic childhood. Do you mind my asking what happened?"

He dismissed the question with a shrug. "I doubt there's anything new I can tell you that hasn't already been reported in newspapers or magazines."

"If you don't want to tell me, I can understand. I don't often talk about my parents' death." She fought to speak through the thickness in her throat. "Or my brother's."

"Ana and I don't share the sort of relationship with the Hollisters that you had with your family." A thread of weariness underscored his comment. "They despise our existence as much as I despise theirs."

Her brows pulled together. "It wasn't their fault, Joc, any more than it was yours and your sister's. There's only one person to blame for this tragedy."

"I'm well aware my father is responsible for the accident of my birth."

There was a bite to his words that should have had her backing off. But for now, she'd follow her instincts. "I'm not sure any of you do realize it. Otherwise there wouldn't be such animosity between all of you." She allowed her fingertips to drift across the hard contours of his bare chest. "What was your father like?"

He caught her hand in his and lifted it to his mouth, kissing each fingertip. "Boss was…charming. Arrogant. Brilliant."

"Sounds familiar."

He released a short, harsh laugh. "You aren't the first to make the comparison. It doesn't help that I look just like him, too."

"And you hate that."

There was an endless pause, and then his voice came out of the silence, low and full of old pain. "I hate most how similar my personality is to his. How close I came to being him. He died in prison, you know. At one point, I thought I might end up there. Die there."

She lifted onto one elbow and stared at him in dismay. "What do you mean? How did you almost end up like him?"

He fell silent for a long moment and then he said, "I was ten when I found out that my father had two families. I saw a news report about him on the television. He stood there posing for the camera, his arm around his wife and his four adorable children lined up in front of him."

"You didn't know before that?" she asked, shocked. "Your mother never told you?"

"She walked into the room just as MacKenzie was answering some question about school. We were in the same grade, and I couldn't understand how that was possible. My mother turned off the set and sat me down and tried to explain. But what could she say? She was the mistress of a married man and nothing was going to change that." He combed his fingers through her hair in a restless movement, though she doubted he even realized he was doing it. "I went a little crazy after that. I started hanging with a bad crowd. There were six of us, including me. Mick, Joey, Peter…and a couple others. Eventually we decided to form a little business partnership."

She shook her head in confusion. "I don't understand. What did that have to do with your father?"

"I decided I'd prove I was every bit the businessman he was. I tried to emulate him, for a while." His voice dropped another notch, the words sounding as if they'd been pulled from some deep, dark place. "Over time, I became him. Shadier, in fact. It was all about the bottom line, financially. All about what I could get away with. All about wheeling and dealing. Nothing else mattered. Not who I ran over to reach my goal. Not the better good. Not finding a balance. The win was everything."

She couldn't help stiffening, remembering something he'd said when they'd first met. *I win. Always. No matter what it takes.* "What's changed since then?"

He understood what she was asking and shrugged. "A lot. I do it aboveboard and I don't cheat. If you sell your ranch it's because I've offered you something you want more than Longhorn."

She took a moment to absorb that. "What convinced you to transform yourself?"

"Not a what, but a who. My sister, Ana. I was a cocky twenty-year-old and she was all of twelve. I bragged to her about this great deal I'd pulled off with Mick and the boys—a scam, really—and she burst into tears. By that time my father's illegal activities had already surfaced, as well as the existence of my mother, and Ana and me. Boss had died in jail the previous year. Ana was terrified that I'd be arrested like our father and she'd be left all alone."

"What about your mother?"

"She was gone, as well. I always felt she'd been hounded to death by the press after the scandal about my father broke." He scrubbed a hand across his jaw. "I guess I felt that since everyone expected me to be my father's son, I would be. Ana made me look—really look—at my life. I made some hard decisions that day."

"What did you do?"

"I ended my association with Mick and the others. From then on, I went out of my way to make sure that every single business deal was scrupulously honest. I went back to school. Eventually I got into Harvard. And I made money. A lot of it."

"And your father's other family? The Hollisters?"

"MacKenzie's mother, Meredith, is a socialite who had the money and the name to match my father's. My mother was a dirt-poor farmgirl from the wrong side of the tracks. He married the one and made a mistress of the other."

"And his children paid the ultimate price."

"Yes." He sat up abruptly, setting the hammock swaying, his face a mask of pain. "I intend to make damn certain history doesn't repeat itself."

"How are you going to do that?" she asked apprehensively.

"It's simple." His eyes turned winter-cold. "I won't have any children. That way I can't screw up their lives."

Four

Joc's remark put a swift end to their interlude on the beach. After they collected their possessions, they returned to the cabaña. Darkness descended, filling the air with new night-blooming scents that were even more intoxicating than those Rosalyn had picked up on during the day. But the mood between her and Joc had changed and she followed him inside without pausing to wallow in the unique fragrances.

"I have nine o'clock reservations at Ambrosia. It's one of the newer hotel restaurants," Joc said. "I suspect you'll be more comfortable using the spare bedroom to freshen up. So take your time getting ready."

She appreciated his consideration in not forcing an unnatural intimacy. She loitered in the shower, and afterward exited into the attached bedroom. To her surprise, a box rested on the bed with her name scrawled on the tag. She examined it with equal parts curiosity and trepidation. Ripping apart the outer wrapping, she tore off the lid of the box and stared at the contents. To call it a dress didn't do it justice. She eased it from its nest of tissue and shook her head in amazement.

The floor-length gown would have been lighter than a feather if it hadn't been for the beadwork. Of course, if it hadn't been for the beadwork, the wearer would have been arrested for public indecency. The black gown was as sheer as a negligee, swirls of beads in the shape of exotic flowers fanning the bodice and curling across the pelvis and buttocks. Two spaghetti straps claimed to hold the gown in place, but Rosalyn suspected they lied.

She gave the gown a light shake and a scrap of paper floated to the ground. It landed faceup on the carpet and she picked it up. *I hope you'll wear this for dinner tonight. No other woman could do it justice.* It was a pretty lie, one she chose to believe for a few, sweet moments. Then she examined the gown again, her brow creasing in a frown.

There were reasons she couldn't wear his gift, even if she were willing to accept such an expensive present, reasons Joc couldn't have possibly guessed. The gown was going back right now. Wistfully she ran a hand across the delicate beadwork. It was so beautiful, so feminine, so…so daring. She shook her head. Not that it mattered. Back it went. The instant, the very moment, the exact second after she tried it on.

Giving in to temptation, she tossed aside the robe

she'd donned after her shower and eased the gown over her head. One quick shimmy had it dropping into place and two cautious steps had her in front of the full-length mirror affixed to the bedroom wall. She shook her head in disbelief. The mundane rancher had been transformed into something…glamorous.

The gown fit as though painted on, clinging to every sleek curve. From the front it had the unmitigated gall to appear modest, the bodice only hinting at cleavage. She suspected the same couldn't be said for the back. Rotating, she examined herself over her shoulder. Holy mother! The gown plunged endlessly, screeching to a halt a scant half inch above the curve of her buttocks. Coiling flower stems outlined in flashing red snaked along the edges of the deep U, drawing the eye on a helpless journey down her spine before arriving at the sassy collection of beads that cupped her bottom.

No way. No way would she wear this gorgeous, outrageous, elegant gown in public, especially since it risked revealing things she'd rather keep concealed. She stepped closer to the mirror, eyeing her abdomen through the beads before turning to check whether anything could be seen along her right hip. To her delight, nothing was visible. As with the one-piece maillot she'd worn to the beach, not a single flaw showed. Oh, dear. It truly was the perfect gown.

Before she could wiggle out of it a knock sounded at the door, and she crossed the room to answer it. From knee to floor, the gown fluttered as she walked, belling outward in flirty wisps. She gave an experimental skip, feeling the most feminine she had in ages—maybe ever.

Of course, it was hard to feel feminine when your typical mode of dress was a sweat-soaked plaid shirt, boots and a pair of worn jeans stained with elements best left unidentified.

She opened the door a scant inch and peeked through the narrow opening. Joc stood there. "I want you to wear it," he said without preliminary.

She gave a short laugh. "One of the saddest aspects of life is that we don't always get what we want."

"What will it take for you to agree?"

She lifted an eyebrow. "Another negotiation?" she asked. "I thought we weren't negotiating on this trip."

"If that's what's necessary to get you into that gown, that's what we'll do."

"Before you try to get me out of it?"

His chuckle was one of agreement, the soft, intimate sound sending an unwanted shaft of desire arrowing through her. "You can't hang a man for dreaming, Red."

"Condemn him, maybe."

"Only if I manage to turn that dream into reality."

She flashed on an image of his powerful hands on her shoulders, snapping the thin straps of the gown. Rapt masculine eyes watching as the weight of the beads sent the dress plummeting to the floor in a glittering pool of black, edged with flaming red. The vulnerability of nudity mixed with a painful, unremitting want. His reaching for her. Her retreat toward the bed. His pursuit. The endless tumble to the waiting mattress. Helpless desire growing with each touch before the inevitable mating of body and soul—

She dismissed that possibility without hesitation,

though something hot and heavy settled deep in the pit of her stomach, something that had the beads of the gown shuddering in agitation. "That's not going to happen," she managed to tell him. Or were her words meant for herself?

"Time will tell. So, are you going to wear it?"

She couldn't resist sneaking another peek over her shoulder, the mirror reflecting an image she'd never seen before. Common sense warred with an irrational, wholly feminine craving. For the past decade, she'd always put the interests of Longhorn ahead of her own. Always. For the first time ever, she wanted to be tempted. Wanted to surrender to the forbidden. To the fantasy in which she found herself.

She spoke before common sense won out, giving way to the baser of her two choices. "I either dine in this or the jeans I wore to fly out here."

"Actually, it's that or your bathrobe since your other clothes are being laundered." His eyes gleamed with laughter at having boxed her in so neatly. "So, will you wear it?"

"I guess I don't have any other choice."

"Not a one," he agreed.

"I do have a request, however."

"Name it."

She glanced down at her toes poking out from beneath the hem of the gown. "I think I'll need more than just this dress. I'm guessing Ambrosia has a policy against dining in bare feet. Unless you want me to wear my boots?"

"Check the box. You'll find shoes and underwear."

Her brows tugged together. "Underwear?"

"Dig around. There are a couple of beads strung together with dental floss that you're supposed to wear under the dress. I'm not surprised you missed it."

She'd been so focused on the gown, she hadn't noticed the shoes, let alone the underwear. She stirred uneasily. "Listen… Just so we're clear. There aren't any strings attached to your gift, right?"

"Only the ones that hold the beads in place." He checked his watch. "If you'll excuse me, I have a brief appointment I can't avoid. Why don't I meet you at Ambrosia at nine?"

"I'll be there."

But even as the words escaped, a part of her warned that she was a fool, allowing herself to be seduced by Joc and his fantasy world. Come tomorrow she'd be back to reality and that transition would come fast and hard…and no doubt as painful as a fall from a bucking stallion.

At precisely nine o'clock, Joc had the intense pleasure of watching Rosalyn stride through Ambrosia toward him. He wasn't the only one watching. Of course, the gown she wore might have played a part in the attention she received. It provided a dramatic contrast to her wine-red hair, pale complexion and spectacular physique. But it was more than the dress. It was the strength of her personality that held everyone's attention—the life force that caused the very air to shimmer around her.

His smile deepened. She truly was glorious. In four-inch heels she appeared downright statuesque. The subdued lighting flashed off the beading of her gown like a series of warning beacons as she cut through the collection of tables blocking her path with a lazy, long-legged grace. Conversation halted briefly at her approach before swelling with her passage. Not that she noticed. Nor did she notice the maître d' scurrying in her wake, outraged that she'd invaded his domain without permission, escort, or so much as a by-your-leave.

Joc stood at her approach, their gazes locking. Eyes as stunning a blue as a deepening sunset regarded him warily. "You look beautiful," he offered.

"Thanks." Her mouth curved to one side as she gave his suit the once-over. "So do you."

Her frankness filled him with a fierce satisfaction. Whatever mysterious quirk of nature had sparked the attraction between them, it was definitely mutual. As hard as she might resist that attraction, what would happen between them had been determined long ago. She could fight the inevitable—no doubt would fight—but ultimately, there'd be no turning from it.

He waited while the maître d' held her chair before taking the seat across from her. She finally became aware of the beleaguered man's presence and flashed him a generous smile that earned her instant forgiveness. Joc concealed his amusement at how sublimely oblivious she was to the undercurrents swirling around her.

Perhaps it was her intense focus on the path she forged through life that kept her from noticing such subtleties. Or perhaps the people who crossed her path sensed what he had when he'd first met her—that she was someone special. Whatever the root cause, the outcome remained the same. Rosalyn left an indelible mark wherever she went, attracting people with effortless ease.

The sommelier arrived just then to discuss the extensive wine list, followed by the waiter, who took several minutes to describe the various dishes and house specials. The instant they'd placed their order, she glanced at him and Joc suddenly realized that she was down-to-the-bones nervous, the emotion implicit in every aspect of her appearance from the flash of flame-red hair and black beads, to the ripple of tension across shoulders and arms that her gown so beautifully revealed.

"What's wrong?" he asked quietly.

She didn't bother dissembling. "I'm just not sure why I'm here."

"You can leave at any time. I told you there weren't any strings involved in our night together and I meant it."

She gave him a direct look. "I can change my mind and you wouldn't be upset?"

Blunt and to the point. He liked that about her. "Disappointed, but not upset." He reached for her hand, pausing just short of touching her in order to make his point. His fingers were splayed so close above hers, that she could feel the warmth, feel the current of attraction that flowed between them. It forged a connection, one she couldn't ignore. "But you won't change your mind."

He caught the slight tremble of her fingers before she steadied them. She was strong-willed, he'd give her that. And tenacious. But no matter how hard she fought to put rationality before emotion, her body betrayed her. All it took was that almost-touch and the heat flared between them. Carefully she slid her hand out from beneath his and rubbed her palm across her thigh, as though attempting to erase her response to him. He doubted she was even aware of her actions. In fact, he knew she wasn't.

As she struggled to regain her equilibrium, a demi-sec Vouvray arrived at their table, along with their appetizer. The platter contained a selection of bite-size delicacies. Ice-cold prawns vied with spiced calamari. Delicate slivers of sautéed scallops were artfully arranged on *galettes au fromage*. And clam-shaped pastry puffs were guarded by stalks of marinated asparagus.

He transferred the most succulent of the selections to her plate while she sampled the wine. Plucking a prawn from her plate, Rosalyn dipped it in the chef's specialty cocktail sauce and took a bite. She closed her eyes and sighed with pleasure. His teeth clamped together at the expression on her face. He wanted her to look at him like that, to lie in his bed with moonlight gilding her nudity and look at him in just that way as he slid inside her. He made a decision there and then. He didn't care what it took. He didn't care what he had to promise. He wanted this woman. And before the night ended, he'd have her.

"Good?" To his relief, she didn't seem to hear the primitive male aggression ripping apart that single word. But she was no one's fool. If he didn't get himself under control—and fast—she'd figure it out. And chances were excellent, she'd flee. If she were smart, she would.

"This is outstanding." She looked at him then, her eyes heavy-lidded and drunk on sensory pleasure. "The best I've ever had were some tiger prawns in New Orleans, but I think there's a new winner in town."

She helped herself to some of the calamari. "So, did you take care of your business?"

He shook his head. "I won't be able to do that until tomorrow morning. My appointment this evening was with my lawyer. Preliminary work before I meet with the other owners of Deseos."

"Huh. It didn't occur to me that you might have partners. I just assumed you were the sole owner of the island." She offered a swift, self-deprecating smile. "Silly, huh?"

"Not at all. As a matter of fact, by the end of tomorrow I *will* be the sole owner."

That stopped her. She returned the scallops she'd been about to sample to her plate. "That sounds ominous."

He shrugged. "The partnership didn't work out. I should have known, based on our past history."

Her eyes narrowed as she worked her way through his deliberately oblique comment, dissecting it bit by bit. "By any chance are we talking about Mick and your other school friends?"

She was quick, he'd give her that. "The very same."

"Why would you—" She broke off. "I'm sorry. That's none of my business."

"No, it's not, but I'll answer, anyway." He couldn't keep the hard quality from infiltrating his voice. "Mick and the others came to me, all of them together like the band of brothers we'd once been. They claimed they'd fallen on hard times. Made bad choices in their lives. They said they'd finally come around, just as I had all those years ago, and were ready to change. All they needed was a helping hand. Of course, that wasn't what they were after."

"What were they after?" she asked softly.

"Deseos, of course." He bit off the end of a bread-stick and crushed it between his back teeth. "And the opportunity to screw me over because I'd left them behind all those years ago. Left them behind and made my fortune without them."

Noting her shock, he abandoned the subject and moved the conversation to more neutral topics. He wanted the night to revolve around romance, not dissention. To entice her, not scare her off. The rest of the evening passed with surprising ease, the discussion flowing from one topic to the next. He found Rosalyn an intriguing companion, sharp, witty and one of the most confident women he'd ever met. He couldn't remember the last time he'd met someone so comfortable in her own skin, so aware of who she was and where she came from.

After they'd finished their dinner, Joc suggested a walk on the pier, an offer Rosalyn accepted with alacrity. They wandered through the hotel garden and he mated his stride to hers, not quite touching, but close enough to catch her unique fragrance and feel the warmth of her body.

They reached the pier and she struggled to deal with the uneven planking in the ridiculous shoes he'd bought for her. She only stumbled once, but it was enough to elicit a hiss of annoyance from him. He cut in front of her. The instant she checked up, he crouched at her feet.

"Hang on a sec. You're going to break an ankle in those things and I'll be to blame. Let me get them off you."

Encircling her ankle, he lifted her foot across his thigh. His fingers were warm and careful, caressing the sensitive skin around her ankle with a feather-light touch. Rosalyn held herself rigidly erect, feeling like the world's most awkward stork. Teetering, she doubled over and clamped onto his shoulders. He shot out a hand to steady her, cupping her hip. His fingers splayed across the curve of her backside, his thumb following the line of the single elastic thread—dental floss, he'd called it—that held her thong in place. He lingered, stroking for a brief, delicious instant.

The sizzle from that stolen caress burned through the thin material of her gown, igniting a shock wave that caused every bead on her dress to glitter in distress. He lifted his head, his face only inches from hers. She could hear the rasp of his breath, fast and rough. Feel his desire. Practically taste the urgency that flowed between them. It was wrong, wrong in every possible way. Even knowing that, her hold on him gentled, eased from grip to embrace. She wanted to fall into him. Consume him. Battle toward the sweetest of surrenders. His name escaped of its own volition, hovering in the air between them.

He responded by reaching out and stroking her bottom lip with his thumb. "Soon," he murmured.

The promise broke whatever spell she'd been under and she eased back, suddenly self-conscious. "There's no rush."

"So I've been telling myself. Based on our reaction to each other, I'm not convinced that's true." He finished removing her shoe before following suit with the second, his touch more impersonal, as though that moment of desperate awareness had never happened. Standing, he hooked the heels over the lip of his pocket. "Ready?" he asked.

She snatched a quick, steadying breath and nodded. "I can walk, if that's what you mean." Barely.

Get a grip! she ordered herself as she headed toward the end of the pier. What was wrong with her that the instant he came too close she lost every intelligent thought she possessed? Did she want him to kiss her? Did she hope to use that kiss as an excuse? An excuse to what? Fall mindlessly into his arms? To have a one-night stand with him and be done with it? She couldn't say for certain, which only served to alarm her all the more. She was losing control, something she couldn't afford to do.

Once she left fantasyland she had a ranch to consider—and a man with the drive to win at all costs intent on wrestling it away from her. She couldn't afford to lose herself in a sexual haze while he busied himself working out a plan for circumventing her and achieving his goal.

She had to remember it was her duty to protect her land at all costs. It was part of her heritage, part of the Oakley legacy that had been passed from generation to generation for nearly a hundred and eighty years. Maybe if she focused on that, on her need to protect her ranch by uncovering Joc's weaknesses, she'd find a way to get through the rest of the evening.

Small groups pocketed the lighted boardwalk, some fishing, some wrapped in an embrace, others just gazing out at the ocean. She walked in silence until they could go no farther. No one else had ventured quite this far, and she paused beneath the circle of light cast from a wrought-iron lamp.

"What's wrong?" he asked.

She didn't bother prevaricating. "I'm just wondering why I agreed to come here with you." She swept a hand downward to indicate her gown. "What am I doing here, dressed like this, intent on having a one-night stand with you?"

"Have you changed your mind?"

She glanced at him. "Have you?"

"Not even a little."

"I want you," she admitted with devastating honesty. "But I'm not sure how smart it is to give in to that want when it might put my ranch in jeopardy."

"You don't trust me."

She shook her head. "No more than you trust me. Or your old friends. Or the Hollisters." She fixed him with an unflinching stare. "So, why am I here, Joc? What do you really want? Is this your way of romancing the ranch out from under me?"

"Damn it, Red." Ripe frustration underscored his words. "You know what I want, and right now it has nothing to do with your ranch. I want you in my bed. I want to make love to you until neither of us can think straight."

An image of them together flashed through her mind. It came easily. Too easily. The sounds, the scents, the feel of him over and around and inside of her. The breeze tugged at her hair, kicking free a silken strand. It danced around her face, highlighting her agitation. "And afterward?"

He fought to clamp down on his emotions, and she marveled at his struggle. It was an impressive one. "Afterward, we're back where we started," he admitted through gritted teeth. He approached, halting a scant foot away. Without her heels, he towered over her. For the first time in more years than she could recall, she felt small and vulnerable and unsure of herself. "Does that even matter? If we both agree that whatever happens tonight has nothing to do with our business association—"

She cut him off without hesitation. "We don't have a business association."

"I repeat. Then where's the problem? You want me. I want you. Your ranch has nothing to do with what's happening between us. All we have to do is return to the cabaña. Agree, and we can both have what we want most."

Stepping outside of the circle of lamplight, she tried to separate desire from practicality. Not that she succeeded. Right now she didn't care about the consequences, despite knowing that though this felt right, it was guaranteed to go wrong. "I don't know, Joc. I need to think."

He followed her into the shadows, allowing the darkness to swallow them both. He dropped his hands onto her shoulders. "You chose to come with me. There's only one reason you'd have done that."

Her gaze never left his face. He was right. There was only one reason. More than anything, she wanted this one night in his bed. He must have read her answer in her eyes. He cupped her shoulders and drew her against him. Then he lowered his head and took her mouth with his.

A desperate need raced through her, just as it had when he'd kissed her by the old homestead. The feeling bit just as urgently now as then. Heady desire stole every thought from her head, and drove her to wrap her arms around his neck and pull him closer yet. Her lips parted beneath the insistent pressure of his and his tongue swept inward to duel with hers. He tasted of wine and passion, deliciously warm and moist, gifting her with an intense pleasure unlike anything she'd ever experienced before.

His hands slid from her shoulders downward, tracing her back where her gown bared her. She shuddered beneath the teasing caress. Unable to help herself, she pressed closer, feeling the unyielding ridge of his arousal. She needed to touch him, to forge a more intimate contact. She found him with her hands, cupping him through the trousers of his suit. He groaned, the sound rough and primal, and she made her decision.

"Please take me back to the cabaña," she whispered against his mouth.

Without a word, he took her hand in his and retraced their steps. The walk to the owner's suite seemed endless. She didn't dare pause to admire the scenery. She simply focused on putting one bare foot in front of the other and moving forward with all due diligence and speed until they found themselves standing in the foyer of Joc's cabaña.

He didn't say a word. He didn't have to. His eyes said it all. He stared down at her for an endless moment with a gaze that reflected moon-drenched nights filled with unforgettable passion. Reality faded beneath that look, tempting her to indulge in pure physical pleasure.

But she couldn't, not entirely. She was too pragmatic

for fantasy and had faced too many painful endings to believe that a single night of desire could lead anywhere but to another painful ending. Even knowing all that, she still couldn't resist the inevitable, though she'd do her best to make that ending a little less painful.

She moistened her lips. "If we...if we—"

"Make love."

"It's not making love. It's sex," she insisted, before plowing onward. "If we have sex, I need you to understand that it has nothing to do with the ranch or our negotiations."

"I know."

"I don't use sex as a tool. I never have and I never will."

He dropped her shoes and tipped her face up to his. "Listen to what I'm saying, Red." His hands sank deep into her hair. "I know you don't. That you wouldn't."

"I just needed to make that clear." She snatched a quick breath and forced herself to admit the truth, more for her own benefit than for his. "I want you. Physically. And then I want to walk away and never see you again."

He shook his head. "That's not going to happen."

"Those are the only rules I can live with. One time," she negotiated desperately. "Then never again."

"You're about to discover that I'm a man who breaks all the rules." He feathered a kiss across her mouth, eliciting a helpless moan. "Our first time will be tender and slow and as prolonged as I can make it."

She moaned again. "You just want to make me suffer."

"I plan to do my very best. And it won't be one time. It'll be all night long. By the time we're through, we'll be so intertwined we won't be able to tell where one of us begins and the other ends."

If he hadn't been holding her up, she would have melted into a puddle at his feet. "And then we walk away." Assuming they could still walk. "After we get untwined, we go our separate ways, right?" She had to win one concession in this devil's bargain, because she'd fast come to realize that, like it or not, they were in the middle of an intense negotiation.

"That might be a little difficult considering we're on an island. We still have to fly home together tomorrow."

"But after that. Never again. We part company. Otherwise…otherwise no sex." Who was she kidding?

His grin flashed in the darkness. "I guess there's not much I can do about it, if that's what you want."

"That's what I want. One night and after that we're through with each other." And after they returned to Dallas, she'd never see him again. Never allow him to touch her again. Never be held in his arms again or shudder in anticipation of what would happen over the coming hours. Her arms tightened around his neck. But that was tomorrow. She still had tonight. "Make love to me, Joc. Quick. Before I change my mind."

Five

Joc lifted Rosalyn with an easy strength. Instead of carrying her to either of the two bedrooms, he headed for the lanai. It was more humid here, but nighttime cool. Lush, delicious scents filled the air, scents that the air-conditioning hadn't scrubbed clean.

He lowered Rosalyn to her feet and she crossed to the screen door and stared out toward the lagoon. Shadows covered much of the view, but she could see the moonlight gleaming on the white-tipped waves as they curled toward shore, and could hear the muted crash as the water pounded the sand, followed by the soft hiss of retreat.

Tonight she intended to be selfish. Tonight was hers. Just this one night, with moonlight drenching them and the stars raining down. Just one night of greed, to take what was offered. To use and be used until she couldn't see or think straight. To have every last problem blown straight out of her head. To have a few hours to herself without worrying about finances, or a broken fence line or sick livestock or promises she was honor bound to keep.

Joc wrapped his arms around her. "Where have you gone, Red?"

She turned in his arms and blew out a sigh. "I'm an idiot."

"Second thoughts?"

She dropped her head to his shoulder. "It's not that." She started to laugh, hoping he didn't hear the heart-break that hid behind her amusement. "This—" She gestured to encompass the room and the island and him. "It's supposed to be a night off. A night of fantasy."

"An escape from reality."

"Yes."

He lifted her chin and grimaced at her expression. "Started thinking, did you?"

"I did." He surprised her by smoothing the furrows from her brow and she relaxed against him. "I don't suppose there's something you can do about that?"

"I'll give it my best shot."

He kissed her. Not with the desperate passion of earlier. Not with a blistering stamp of possession. This was an exploration, a delving into something new and fascinating. Something not to be rushed. Her breathing quickened, as did her want. It rose like the tide, building and curling, a wave of need rushing toward shore. She reached for him as it broke, wrapping her arms tight, tight, tight around his neck. His tongue dueled with hers, teasing, taunting, mating. She couldn't get enough. Not close enough, not hard enough, not…just not enough.

He edged her away from the screen door and deeper into the lanai, deeper into the shadows and the blessed darkness. She felt his hands in her hair. Felt the quick tugs as he plucked free the pins holding her hair in place.

"I've wanted to do this all night." Her hair slid downward and he filled his hands with the weighty mass. "Why would you keep something this beautiful hidden away?"

She stared in bewilderment. "It wasn't hidden."

"First that stupid hat."

"It keeps the sun off my face."

"Then tonight."

"I was going for sophisticated. I thought it matched the dress."

His gaze lowered. "Yes. The dress. Let's see what we can do about that."

He slid the spaghetti straps from her shoulders before finding the zip and lowering it. The weight of the beads sent the bodice of the gown dropping. It didn't stop there. It slid all the way to her hips and clung for a brief instant before gravity sent it plummeting to the floor with a nervous chatter of beads.

She stood before him in nothing more than a wispy thong and acres of pale naked skin. Suddenly self-conscious, she shifted so she remained clear of the moonlight, hoping the cloak of shadows hid most of her flaws. "You still have all your clothes on," she said. "That strikes me as patently unfair."

He couldn't take his eyes off her. "I'm forced to

disagree." He cupped her breast and stroked his thumb across the tip. "You're as perfect as I'd anticipated."

She shivered at the agonizing tightening of her nipple, the sensation piercing straight to her core. How could she be wound so tight that every nerve felt on the verge of exploding, while at the same time that single touch had her entire body loosening and softening?

"You didn't have to anticipate too hard." She fought to speak through a haze of desire. "That dress didn't leave much to the imagination."

"Which is why I chose it with you in mind." His voice deepened. "And then, with you out of it in mind."

His fingernail scraped again and she lost it. She yanked at the tie moored at his neck until she'd managed to rip it loose. The buttons of his shirt came next, the studs that held it closed hitting the wooden floor with soft pings as they scattered. She worked her way past his shirt until she reached hot, hard flesh. There she paused, reveling in the feel of him, in the strength and power of endless muscle and sinew. God, he was in incredible shape. She covered him with kisses as she removed each article of clothing.

When he was as naked as she, he backed them toward one end of the lanai to a love seat which he flattened into a daybed. She tumbled backward onto the thick cushions. They were soft and cool against her back and his weight had her sinking into them, the dichotomy of searing and inflexible above, and light and downy beneath, making her head swim.

"Joc!" His name escaped in a desperate rush, pleading for something she couldn't seem to express any other way.

Determination cut across his face and he touched her, soothing without saying a word. His mouth found hers, the joining of lips and tongue filled with a tenderness at odds with the fierceness of his personality. There was a newness to their kiss, as though they'd discovered some fresh and unexpected delicacy and were intent on savoring every moment. She'd never experienced anything like it—lustful, yet sensitive. Passionate, yet poignant.

He cupped her breasts, teasing the peaks before this attention drifted downward. Before she could stop him, his hands swept across her abdomen and he froze. Instantly she blocked his view with her arm, an instinctive attempt at self-preservation.

"No, honey, don't." He interlaced her fingers with his. "You don't have to hide from me."

Rearing back, he shifted her arm to one side so silvered moonlight spilled across her torso, merciless in what it exposed. She stared at the ceiling and the pounding of her heartbeat filled her ears as she waited for his reaction, waited to see if he accepted or rejected her. Then he touched her again, tracing the jagged scar from where it started, just beneath her left breast. Inch by excruciating inch he followed its path across her abdomen to where it terminated, high on her right hip.

She shivered beneath the intimate touch. Other than the physicians who'd treated her, only one other person had ever seen that scar. At the end of their affair, he'd told her he'd made love to her despite it, even though it sickened him to look at it, or to accidentally touch it. But Joc seemed determined to examine every aspect. Just when she was on the verge of erupting off the love seat, he spoke.

"How, Red?" He sounded vaguely outraged. "How did this happen?"

She fought to speak in a normal voice. "It was an accident."

"I'm relieved to hear it wasn't on purpose. But…that must have been some accident."

"It was."

"Aw, hell. This happened when you took over running Longhorn after your parents' death, didn't it? That's when you were scarred."

She nodded. "My first week on the job. I was eighteen and in way over my head. The bull knew it and explained the facts of life to me."

He bit out a curse. "You were gored?"

"Yes. I've carried that scar as a reminder ever since."

"A reminder of what?"

"Of what I owe the legacy I've been given, and the toll that legacy sometimes exacts."

"You're self-conscious about it, aren't you?"

In response, she threw an arm across her face. Her withdrawal stirred an instantaneous reaction. He lowered his head and his ebony hair caressed her belly, his breath warming her chilled skin. And then his mouth closed over the scar. A shudder erupted from deep inside, directly beneath his lips, spreading outward in surges of liquid heat.

"I hate that this happened to you," he murmured. "But what I hate worse is that it's stolen your self-confidence and made you uncertain at a moment when you should be at your most powerful. When you should be the most secure in your femininity."

His words slipped deep into her soul, thawing something that had long been frozen. Tears filled her eyes and tracked a silent path along her temples and into her hair. "I thought it might repulse you."

He looked at her, a look that allowed her to see deep inside, to know that when he spoke it was with absolute honesty and sincerity. "This is a mark of survival. How could it repulse me?"

She didn't know how long she lay there, absorbing the shock of his words. All she knew was that he'd stripped her bare, uncovering the one place she was most vulnerable. He was her enemy, and she'd exposed her wounded underbelly. But instead of taking advantage of her defenselessness, instead of ripping her to shreds, he'd given her back her strength. She reached for him, determined to match strength for strength, to give as he had.

She cupped his face and tugged him back into her arms. He kissed her, his mouth warm and demanding, welcoming her inward. She wrapped herself around him, staking a claim.

"Please, Joc." She lifted her hips in a suggestive swirl. "I want you."

When he refused to take their embrace further, she seized the initiative. She gently scored his chest with her nails before trailing her fingertips across his rippled abs. And then she dipped lower still, cupping the very source of his desire. His breath escaped in a harsh gasp.

"Are you trying to kill me, woman?" The question burst from between clenched teeth.

"Not kill you. Not quite." She peeked up at him with a teasing grin. "Do you like it?"

"Oh, yeah." He caught hold of her wrists and pulled them above her head, anchoring them there with one hand. "Now let's see how you like it."

He cupped the moist delta between her legs, dipping inward in slow, teasing strokes. He didn't stop until she was arching beneath his touch, pleading for his possession. Not that it helped. She could feel herself losing control, her muscles clenching and fluttering on the verge of climax. She lay beneath him, open and wanting. As though sensing how close to the edge she hovered, he slipped between her legs.

"This was inevitable from the beginning," he told her, as he reached for protection. "From the moment I first saw you, I knew it could only end one way."

"Then let it end," she begged.

There was no more talking after that. He joined them, sheathing himself in her heat with a single powerful stroke. What came next was a primal dance as old as time.

She rode the moment, wishing it could last forever. But she was too close to the edge for that to happen. The fluttering began again, rippling and fisting. Joc threw back his head, his throat moving convulsively as he drove home. And then the rapture came, overwhelming in its intensity.

Rosalyn had thought this night would be a simple sexual act. But in that timeless instant, where two became one, in that moment of perfect union, what she felt grew into something far deeper. Something that bonded her to him. Something that forever changed her.

Far worse, it became something she knew with absolute certainty she'd never be able to walk away from.

* * *

Joc watched, once again, as Rosalyn slowly woke. As before on the plane, her sleepy expression held a heart-wrenching vulnerability, one that cut him to the quick. All of her secrets were exposed to his scrutiny—the helpless passion he'd roused in her. The physical scar she'd hidden from him so self-consciously. The emotional scars she protected with even greater care. And worst of all, the events that had transpired just a few short hours ago. It was all there in the nervous caution with which she regarded him.

"Morning," he greeted her, the word taking on a gruff quality.

She eased upward, pulling the sheet to her chin. "Morning." She closed her eyes and released a chagrined laugh. "Listen to us. Considering what happened last night—"

"Not to mention this morning."

Her gaze clashed with his at the reminder. "Not to mention this morning," she confirmed with impressive calm. "After all that you'd think we'd be more comfortable with each other."

"Speaking of this morning…" He watched the color come and go in her cheeks. "I seem to recall we were unfortunate enough to have a slight equipment malfunction."

"You mean—"

He didn't temper his words. "I mean, the condom broke. Are you on the pill?"

She shook her head. "There's never been any need."

"Then we have a problem."

The sophisticated woman from the night before

vanished beneath the unrelenting tropical light of day. She sank deeper into the pillows, shadows darkening her eyes, and pulled her legs tight against her chest. "There's every chance it isn't a problem," she insisted. But he could hear the note of uncertainty coloring her declaration.

He forced himself to use a calm, reassuring tone of voice, the one that had always brought him the most success during tense negotiations. "I assume we won't know for a few weeks."

Her confession barely topped a whisper. "No."

"Are you in the middle of your cycle or toward one end?"

"Middle."

He scrubbed his hand across his face. "Okay. There's nothing we can do about it at this point, but I'd like to make a simple request."

"I'm almost afraid to ask… What's your request and how simple is it?"

"I'd like you to promise to call me one way or the other as soon as you know. Will you do that?" He watched her closely, searching for any hint of prevarication. To his relief he saw none.

"Absolutely."

A phone rang deep within the cabaña and with a swift apology, he went to answer it, dealing with details for the upcoming meeting with impatient efficiency. By the time he returned to the lanai, Rosalyn was gone, having used the interruption as an opportunity to escape. Not that he blamed her. No doubt she felt the less said on the subject, the better, as though ignoring it would make it go away.

He stood for a long moment in silent contemplation. A baby. She could be pregnant with his child. He'd always sworn he'd never have children, not after what he and Ana had gone through. But he couldn't get the image of Rosalyn out of his mind. He could see her as clearly as though she were standing there. Strong. Lean. Forthright.

And ripe with his child.

Once again he wanted. Wanted with a passion that defied all attempts at control and threatened all he hoped to achieve.

Rosalyn took her time in the bathroom, scrubbing every inch of herself. But it didn't change anything. Her skin still glowed from Joc's possession, her body forever branded by his touch. She could even smell him, his unique scent lingering on her lips and saturating her senses.

How could she have thought that a single night with him would be sufficient? Last night had been unlike anything she'd ever experienced before, and if she were honest, she'd admit that she wanted more. She'd been a fool to think they'd be able to indulge in a one-night stand and then walk away without consequences, both emotional and...

Her hand slid downward to splay across the flatness of her abdomen. Was it possible? Could she be pregnant? It had only been one slip-up, a slight tear in the "equipment" as Joc referred to it. What were the odds that a baby could result? The probability had to be low. Still... What if it had happened?

She closed her eyes, allowing the hot spray to

cascade over her head. Joc had already made his position perfectly clear. Not only wasn't he interested in having children, but he'd stated in no uncertain terms that he refused to have them. Period. So where did that leave her? Between the proverbial rock and hard place, that's where.

It didn't matter, she decided. If potential became reality, she wouldn't ask Joc for anything. She'd raise the baby on her own. He or she would be an Oakley, with a heritage the child could embrace with pride. The Oakley legacy would continue for another generation. Nothing would make her happier than that.

The water cooled and she hastened to turn it off. She'd wasted enough time. It wasn't in her nature to hide and she wouldn't start now. She'd made a choice last night and she'd face it without flinching. She spared a few minutes to dry her hair and touch up her face with the cosmetics that had been left for her use. She found her clothes from the previous day freshly laundered and folded on the bed. Even her Stetson had been cleaned and blocked. Five minutes later she emerged from the bedroom, ready to face Joc and anything he threw her way.

She found him nursing a cup of coffee, papers spread out on the table in front of him. He stood at her appearance and poured a second cup for her. "How do you take it?"

She gave him the standard Longhorn response. "Black as tar and thick as mud."

That won her a smile. "I have the tar part down, but I'm afraid you'll have to skip the mud and settle for thirty-weight oil."

She returned his smile with one of her own, pleased they were back on a more casual footing. "Not quite as thick, but I'll make do."

"I'm about to head over to the office complex for my meeting." He passed her the coffee. "I'd appreciate it if you'd join me."

His offer caught her off guard. Despite the nonchalant manner in which he'd made the suggestion, she sensed a deeper purpose behind the invitation. She eyed him warily as she downed her coffee. "Just out of curiosity, why would you want me there?"

"I think you'll find it…educational."

She tilted her head to one side, a spark of annoyance flickering to life. "You think I'm in need of an education?"

"When it comes to this particular arena, it wouldn't hurt." He checked his watch. "We'll be leaving for Dallas immediately after I've dissolved the partnership. I should have you home by midafternoon."

Well, what had she expected? That he'd declare his undying love and fix all that had gone wrong in her life? It was a ridiculous dream, particularly when he'd been the one to cause most of her current problems. Besides, she'd been handling endless trials and tribulations for a full decade now. She didn't need a man to rescue her when she was perfectly capable of taking care of herself.

He continued to wait for her response and she gave a brisk nod of her head, hoping she sounded relaxed and easygoing instead of utterly out of her depth. "Fine. I'm always open to new experiences." Not that they'd ever compare to what she'd experienced last night. "I'd find it interesting to sit in on one of your meetings."

As soon as they finished breakfast, they headed over to another rambling building almost identical to the cabaña on the outside, but which bore the undeniable stamp of a business complex once they stepped across the threshold. A secretary ushered them to the conference room, one that didn't share any of the features or characteristics of its counterpart in Dallas.

Light and airy, it reflected the colors and qualities of the island. A plush white carpet the exact shade of the local sand stretched beneath her feet, while the walls were a rich aquamarine that perfectly matched the crystalline water of the lagoon she'd enjoyed the previous day. Instead of a long, rectangular conference table, this one was round, appealing and convivial. It was a room meant to soothe, to allay worry and concern and instill warmth and camaraderie. Or so she thought, right up until she saw the mosaic wolf motif that decorated the surface of the table.

Memories of her first confrontation with Joc came storming back. It made for a harsh transition from the lovemaking they'd shared the previous night to the hard, cold business venue of today. She'd had her romantic interlude. It was over. Bringing her here told her more clearly than words that they were back on a business footing. The time had come to switch gears. Fast.

She glanced around the room, noticing for the first time a group of five suits-and-ties. They stood bunched on one side of the room, helping themselves to coffee and pastries. They chatted in perfect accord, their ease with one another speaking of long acquaintance. So this was Joc's childhood gang. Next to him, they looked normal, average even. They didn't resonate with Joc's unique power or brilliance. Or sexual chemistry. She wondered which one was Mick. She'd find out soon enough, considering he'd probably take the lead opposing Joc during the meeting.

Reluctantly her gaze switched to Joc and she tensed. He'd taken up a stance on the opposite side of the room. He leaned against a sideboard, his full attention focused on the men, while his eyes gleamed with hungry intent. Oh, man. They were clueless. Utterly clueless to their impending doom. They might as well have "Free Rabbit Meat, Bite Here" stamped on their backsides. And though Joc's posture remained relaxed, she could see him gathering himself in preparation for the takedown. Even his features appeared different, the skin taut across his cheekbones, his mouth and jaw set at an angle that shouted a warning to those astute enough to listen.

Then Joc turned to look at her. To her consternation she realized the predator remained. Only now it prowled in her direction. His black eyes glittered with the intensity of it. A memory of the last time they'd made love dwelt there, an acknowledgment of how it had changed them, as well as a promise that soon—very soon—he'd deal with her, too. Where had her lover gone? she wondered in dismay. Or had that man been no more than an illusion?

He caught her stare and indicated a chair apart from the table. "Why don't you sit there?"

"Out of the line of fire?"

He smiled at the dry tone. "Something like that."

As soon as he had her settled, he crossed to the table

and took a seat. The men took their time joining him. From their quick, sidelong glances Rosalyn knew it was a deliberate maneuver. What benefit they thought it gained—other than to tick Joc off—she couldn't imagine. Or maybe that was the point. A subtle power move. "We may be on your turf," they seemed to be saying, "but we're in charge." They had a lot to learn.

One by one they gathered at the table, still conversing among themselves. Next, they took their time arranging their papers. When they were through, a small stack rested before each man, while the expanse of table in front of Joc remained pristine.

"Well, Arnaud," the leader of the group began. Mick, no doubt. "I think this may be the first time you've ever lost. If it makes you feel any better, at least it'll be some of your oldest friends who take you down."

Rosalyn flinched. Was that how she'd sounded when she'd confronted Joc? Was this how she'd appeared, like these foolish rabbits, intent on tweaking the nose of Mr. Big Bad? Heaven help them. And heaven help her.

Joc leaned back in his chair. "What exactly is it I'm about to lose, Mick?" he asked, confirming his opponent's identity.

The men exchanged quick grins. "Isla de los Deseos," Mick said. "We've voted and it's unanimous. We've cut you a check for your share of the partnership. It's nowhere near the value the island will have once we're done developing it, but it is what the agreement calls for."

To Rosalyn's amazement, Joc didn't appear upset by the news. If anything, he seemed…amused. "I assume this is because I wouldn't agree to your plans?"

"We've tried to explain countless times," Mick said. "This place is a gold mine. All we have to do is mine it."

"You mean cover it from end to end with resorts."

"Exactly." A hint of resentment crept into Mick's voice. "You have all the money you could ever want. What's wrong with some of your old gang getting our fair share? It's just one island."

"And the indigenous life?"

"There are other islands. Let them find one of those."

"We've known each other since we were kids, Mick."

Rosalyn caught an odd quality in Joc's voice. A containment that she recognized because she used that same tone whenever she tried to hide her own pain. It took every ounce of self-possession to remain seated and keep her emotions in check when what she really wanted to do was leap from her chair and rush to Joc's side. To throw her arms around him and offer some form of comfort.

"You'd end our friendship over money?" Joc continued. "Or should I say, over more money?"

Mick stared at Joc as though he'd lost his mind. "Hell, yes. Since we need a unanimous vote to develop the island any further, and we can't get a unanimous vote without ousting you…" He tapped the stack of papers in front of him. "You see our dilemma."

"This partnership deal was supposed to help you get back on your feet. All of you."

Mick's hands collapsed into fists. "And now that we're on our feet, we want more. You should understand that. That need for more is what's driven you all these years. You can't deny that."

Joc didn't argue the point. "You do realize I crafted our partnership deal with great care," he said instead.

Mick shook his head. "Not enough care, Joc. You left a clause in there where we could buy you out." He shrugged. "Guess you were feeling altruistic since we were all friends."

"I wouldn't call it altruistic, or even generous. It was more along the lines of…curiosity."

Rosalyn closed her eyes. She had a sneaking suspicion she knew where Joc was going with this. From everything he'd said, he'd been taught at an early age to distrust, even those closest to him. How must it feel to have that distrust confirmed, and all because of money?

Mick leaned back in his chair, attempting to school his face to patience. "What were you curious about?" He didn't really care about Joc's answer, that much was clear. "What could make you so curious you'd be willing to go into a partnership deal with us, particularly one that gave us the upper hand?"

"I was curious to see if you'd screw me over. And you've answered that question."

A hint of red crept into Mick's face. "Glad to help," he growled. "Now let's get this over with."

"Yes, let's. I've arranged for the five of you to leave the island within the hour."

"You don't own the island anymore, Arnaud." Apprehension bled into Mick's fury, giving it a strident edge. "We voted. You're out."

"Read the partnership agreement more carefully.

Hire a lawyer." Joc's gaze shifted down the line of men to the smallest one at the far end. "A real lawyer who specializes in corporate law and partnership agreements rather than hit-and-run cases. He'll be able to point out this small clause I buried in our contract. One you'll find impossible to break. If you vote to remove me as a partner and it's unanimous, I reserve the right to buy out your shares." He checked his watch. "I have better things to do with my time than find where the lawyers put it, but it's there somewhere. Now, if we're through here?"

All four turned to confront the man at the end, the one Rosalyn assumed was the lawyer who specialized in hit-and-run cases. He shrank in his seat. "I didn't see anything," he mumbled. "MacKenzie never said—"

It was as though the air had been sucked from the room. "MacKenzie?" Joc repeated sharply. "She's involved in this? How?"

No one said a word. The men's gazes dropped to the papers in front of them and stayed there. Rosalyn watched Joc struggle with his fury, gather it up and tuck it away behind a growing wall of disillusionment. Once he'd regained his self-control, he addressed the five.

"One more thing," he said, his voice barely above a whisper. "I wasn't going to enforce the second half of that clause I inserted in our contract. But now that I know that MacKenzie's involved in what you're trying to pull, and that you betrayed me by going along with her plan, I've changed my mind. Not only do I have the right to buy out your shares, but it's at the original buy-in price. None of you will see one dime of profit from this place."

"What the hell—"

Joc shoved back his chair and stood. "Trying to stage a coup out of greed is one thing. I can almost understand that," he bit out. "But you brought a Hollister into this. You allowed her to get to me through all of you. No one does that and profits from it."

All hell broke loose after that. It took a full hour for the shouting to die down. The team of lawyers who swept in and gave an explanation of page, line and verse of the buried clause helped bring the disastrous meeting to a close. When it was over, there were no winners as far as Rosalyn could tell. The partners had lost their bid to take over Deseos. But Joc had lost something far more valuable—his friends. Worse, he'd lost the ability to trust, if he'd ever possessed that quality. She suspected he never had or he wouldn't have buried that clause in the partnership agreement.

She realized something else. She'd been invited to witness that scene for a reason. It was Joc's version of a warning. Cross me at your own risk. He didn't lose. Nor did it matter who he took down—friend or foe, it was all the same to him. She'd been the one to insist the previous night remain outside the scope of their business relationship. Today, he proved that wouldn't be a problem.

At least, not for him.

Six

The minute the meeting ended, Joc escorted her straight to the jet. She waited until they were aboard and in their seat with their seat belts fastened before speaking.

"I'm sorry, Joc," she said.

"For what?" But he knew. She could see the bleakness of that knowledge gathering in his eyes.

"Is there anyone in your life you can trust?"

He hesitated before shrugging. "My sister, Ana."

"Ana. The one who lives in Verdonia. How often do you get to see her?"

His expression remained impassive, but she caught the flicker of pain before it vanished behind a facade of indifference. "Whenever I feel like flying out there."

Her heart went out to him. "You're all alone now, aren't you? Instead of having Ana in your corner, she's moved thousands of miles away. She's married to a prince and has a fabulous life. One you aren't part of. It isn't the two of you against the world, anymore, is it?"

"Don't."

He spoke just that one word, but it told her more about him than anything he'd said until this point. Anguish bled through his voice, as well as an immeasurable loneliness. He had no one. He'd cut himself off from personal connections, all because he couldn't trust. She grieved for him, grieved for all he lacked in his life. He'd chosen that path of solitude, whereas it had been thrust on her. Even so, she had friends and neighbors and ranch hands, not to mention Claire. Until last year she'd also had her grandmother. But the main difference between them was that she trusted each and every one of those she'd included in her life. They were as close to her as family.

"We have a problem, Joc. And I don't see an easy solution to it."

He fixed her with his dark gaze, throwing up barriers so high and dense that she didn't have a hope of penetrating them. "What problem?"

"If I'm pregnant, you're going to have to let me in. And if not me, you'll need to open yourself up to our child. Otherwise, how will his relationship with you be any different than your relationship with Boss?"

There was nothing left to say after that and Rosalyn closed her eyes and pretended to sleep. She wished she could nod off. She hadn't slept much last night and she'd have to hit the ground running the instant she arrived in Dallas. She didn't want to think about all the work that had accumulated while she'd been busy playing the role of billionaire's mistress.

To her surprise she did nod off at some point, waking with a soft moan to Joc's distinctive touch. She wanted to blame the way she responded to him on being in that helpless realm between dreams and reality. But in truth, she leaned into him, softened against him, lifted her mouth for his possession for one reason and one reason only.

She wanted him still.

She wanted him on the most visceral level possible, a level that ignored logic and common sense. A primitive, physical level that demanded a taking she could no longer have.

"Wake up, Red." A gentleness slid through his words that confused her since she knew he wasn't a gentle man. "We need to talk."

Catching back another moan, she forced her eyes open. He crouched beside her seat, leaning in so close that all she had to do was bridge that scant inch gap and her mouth would meld with his. She moistened her lips and watched the darkness in his eyes ignite.

"Are we there?" she asked. The words had a sleep-roughened edge, one that seemed to affect him all the more. "I can't believe I slept again."

"We just landed." A swift smile softened the harsh contours of his face, an intimate, revealing smile. Then the mask slammed back into place and he was the Joc from the boardroom once more. "We need to talk," he repeated.

She levered her seat upright, forcing him to shift back. To her relief, it gave her more breathing room. "What do we need to talk about?" she asked. As if she didn't know.

"I'm going to leave instructions with Maggie, my personal assistant, to put you through anytime you call. Don't hesitate to make that call if you need me. For anything."

"Including an unexpected pregnancy?"

His mouth kicked to one side. "Especially that."

There wasn't time to speak after that. The plane door opened to glaring Dallas sunshine and sweltering humidity. Nearby two vehicles sat idling, a familiar-looking limo and a private car. Five minutes later found Rosalyn settled in the car, battered Stetson in hand. Joc leaned in, his smoldering gaze resting first on her face before sliding pointedly to her abdomen. And then he shocked her by taking her mouth in a kiss as hungry and passionate as any she'd received during their night together.

"I'll be expecting your call," he said. And then he left her and crossed to his limo.

Tears pricked Rosalyn's eyes as she watched him drive away. What was wrong with her? She should be delighted to have him out of her life. She didn't need the complications he represented. And she sure as hell didn't need any more on her plate—such as the unplanned advent of a child.

But that didn't stop her from dreaming. Dreaming of a life that had Joc smiling at her the way he had right before he'd taken her in his arms. It didn't stop her from dreaming of holding a baby in her arms, his tiny head thick with hair as black as his father's and eyes the same rich ebony. To have a home that didn't echo with painful memories, but one filled with the laughter and joy of a husband and children. To have the legacy continue. To watch the roots she'd sunk deep in Texan soil grow and expand and shoot toward the sun with endless branches peopled with endless future generations.

Picking up her hat, she dropped it on her head at an angle that had the brim covering her face. Then, leaning back against the plush seat, she allowed the tears to come.

Joc crossed to his limo and climbed into the back, forcing himself not to watch as the car carrying Rosalyn swept off the tarmac and headed away from Dallas toward her ranch. What the hell was wrong with him? He should be grateful to have her out of his life. He didn't need the complications she wrought. And he certainly didn't need the possibility of her carrying his child.

But that didn't stop him from imagining. Imagining a life that had Rosalyn smiling up at him in bed. It didn't stop him from imagining a baby in his arms, her tiny head thick with hair as red as her mother's. To finally know a home of joy and laughter…his wife and children eager to greet him each night. To have the legacy that had always been beyond his reach.

He'd been denied that possibility his entire life. And he'd convinced himself he didn't want it. But now… The limo slowed as it approached Arnaud's, the glass and chrome building stabbing skyward like a finger raised in defiance. Cold, haughty, a safe and remote citadel.

That's what he wanted. Not a worn-down ranch run by a far too discerning redhead. He wanted power and control. But perhaps he'd find a way to have Rosalyn, too.

* * *

Rosalyn stood in the bathroom and read the directions to the home pregnancy test for the third time, determined not to make any mistakes. It appeared straightforward enough. Take the test and a few minutes later the little window would either give her a plus sign if her interlude with Joc three weeks ago had borne fruit, or a negative sign if she was just running unusually late. She followed the instructions to the letter and stood impatiently, her stomach in knots as she waited to learn her fate.

The uncertainty left her feeling like her life was spinning out of control. She longed for stability. For security. To not constantly be teetering on the knife's edge of disaster. The past three weeks had been the most difficult of her life. There hadn't been ten minutes straight over all those days where thoughts of Joc hadn't slipped into her head and left her staring into space, gripped by a longing she couldn't escape.

The small timer she'd set to warn her when the results of the pregnancy test were ready to be read gave off a strident ping. She picked up the plastic stick. A large plus sign showed in the window and she sagged against the sink. Dear God, she was pregnant. She should be horrified. She should be terrified. In a panic. Her brows drew together. Why wasn't she in a panic?

Her hand stole across her abdomen. Her baby grew here, nestled deep within her womb. Hers and Joc's. She wasn't panicked, she realized, any more than she was horrified or terrified. Rather, wonder filled her. A child. Dear heaven, she'd been given a child. She'd been given the chance to have a family again. The tears came then, but to her amazement, she discovered they weren't tears of despair or fear.

They were tears of gratitude.

"Rosalyn!" Claire's shout echoed up the steps, filled with a rare alarm. "Get down here. Fast!"

Escaping the bathroom, Rosalyn pelted down the stairs. She hit the hallway outside the dining room and stumbled on the loose carpet runner, almost taking a nosedive into the sunken living room. The close call scared her, and she pressed a hand to her belly. Time to get that stupid thing tacked down. It wasn't just her neck at risk anymore. She had a baby to consider now.

Claire joined her in the hallway. "What happened?" Rosalyn demanded. "What's wrong? Are you hurt?"

"The barn," Claire gasped. "The barn's on fire."

The next several hours were the worst in recent memory. Thanks to the fast reaction of her employees, they were able to save the horses stabled there. But they weren't able to save the structure, despite a near heroic attempt. Exhausted, choking on smoke and covered with soot, they all grouped together in grim exhaustion. Her foreman pulled her to one side while Claire served cooling draughts of water and platters of sandwiches.

"I think you need to call someone."

Exhaustion had her frowning in bewilderment. "What are you talking about? Call who?"

"When we lost those cows, I wrote it off as bad luck. Downed lines, it happens. Calves gone missing, questionable but not necessarily criminal activity. But there's no question anymore, Rosalyn. That fire was set. Deliberate. Somebody's sending you a message. I suggest you find out who and do something about it."

She stared, stunned. "No. You must be mistaken."

"There's no mistake. The place reeked of gasoline." The foreman wiped his face with the sleeve of his shirt, smearing a trail of soot across his forehead. "We're lucky we saved the livestock. Next time we might not be so lucky."

"Who would do such a thing?"

"Only one person I know who wants to get his hands on this place."

She shook her head, refusing to believe it. "No. It couldn't be Joc."

Granted, he wanted her property. Even so, he'd never stoop to something like this. Not the man who'd held her in his arms and made love to her all through the night. That man wouldn't treat her with such ruthless disregard. And he sure as hell wouldn't put her in danger—or the child he knew she might be carrying.

But maybe he could help her find out who was responsible. "I'll deal with it."

"Soon?"

"Right now," she promised.

She started toward her Jeep, only to realize that she'd parked it in its usual spot beneath the barn overhang. It stood amidst the smoldering ruins, gutted by the fire. That hurt almost as much as losing the barn. Her father had used that Jeep to teach her to drive. It had been a connection to him over the years, his memory with her each time she bumped and ground her way across Oakley land. Setting her jaw, she spun in her tracks and crossed to the pickup Duff used for his mail runs.

Time to face the man who'd turned her life upside down and who'd crept into her heart and mind and soul. A man she longed to have in her life for more than a single night. To find out if he were the man she remembered from Deseos…or the man who put business ahead of every other consideration.

Time to face the father of her baby.

Joc stood at the window of his office and stared out at the sprawling metropolis before him. Heat shimmered beyond the tinted glass, giving the air a heavy fluidness, as though he rested underwater rather than high above the earth.

Damn it! How was it possible that out of all the women he'd ever known, Rosalyn was the only one capable of tying him up in knots? Granted, she was beautiful. Dynamic, and then some. Opinionated. Bullheaded. Glorious. Radiant. And the most passionate of any woman he'd ever held in his arms. He'd never been so distracted by a woman—never allowed a woman to distract him. But this one… What was it about this one?

He couldn't count the number of times he'd picked up the phone, intent on calling her, on demanding she come to him. Nor could he count the number of times he'd instructed his driver to take him out to the Oakley homestead, only to rescind the order an instant later. As if she, alone, weren't distraction enough, a strong possibility existed that she carried his child. Otherwise, why hadn't she called to tell him they were in the clear?

If she was pregnant, there'd be only one resolution to the situation. Only one resolution he'd allow, regardless of Rosalyn's opinion on the matter.

"Joc?"

He stiffened at the sound of his assistant's voice. Hell. He hadn't even heard her enter, which told him how bad the problem had become. Gathering his self-control like a cloak, he turned to face her. "Yes, Maggie? What is it?"

"I was about to go to lunch when security called. They're detaining a woman who's insisting on seeing you immediately. I had them send her up. It's…it's Rosalyn Oakley."

A hungry grin slashed across Joc's face. "Thank you, Maggie. I'll handle it. You can go to lunch."

Red had returned. And this time he wouldn't be so foolish as to let her go. Before the day ended, he'd have her back where she belonged. In his bed. He wanted her. She wanted him. What could be easier? They'd work through whatever peculiar chemical reaction had them panting after one another. Clearly it needed longer than a single night to excise from their systems. Now that he'd had time to consider the matter, he doubted anything short of a full-blown affair would be suffi-cient. And if there was a baby?

They'd find a way to deal with that, too.

The door into the office opened. And there she was in all her glory. She must have been in a hurry coming here because she hadn't dressed for the occasion, as most women confronting a former lover would have. Not a scrap of makeup touched the porcelain surface of her face. He frowned. In fact, it looked like she'd fallen headfirst into a coal mine. Her hair escaped its customary knot, drifting untidily to her shoulders. Just as she had the first time they'd met, she'd dressed in utilitarian ranch gear, jeans and a plaid shirt. But she must have been in a serious hurry, since she'd snapped her shirt together wrong and her clothes were smudged with soot.

Soot!

"What happened?" he asked sharply.

She answered with typical bluntness, giving it to him straight. "My barn burned down."

For most of his life Joc had been described as a brilliant tactician, a man who never allowed emotion to cloud his judgment. He'd always maintained impeccable control and timing. But in the space of two seconds flat Rosalyn Oakley managed to vanquish every ounce of his control and timing as his emotions streaked out of control.

He crossed the room in a half dozen swift steps and grasped her arms, sweeping her with an all-encompassing look. "Are you injured? Were you hurt?"

She shook her head. "I'm fine. Tired. Dirty. But fine."

"Your men? Your animals?"

"All safe." She gazed up at him, her violet-blue eyes reflecting a worrying combination of anger and fear. "Someone burned it down, Joc. On purpose. And there've been other problems, as well. Cut fence lines. Cows taking sick. Calves gone missing. But it wasn't until today that my foreman was certain that it was deliberate."

He froze, suspicion crashing over him. Did she think he was involved? Was that why she'd approached him after three weeks of silence? "And you came here because…?"

She stiffened ever so slightly. "You said to contact you if I needed you. For anything. Were you just saying that, or did you mean it?"

"I meant it."

Relief spread across her face and she swayed toward him before catching herself. Extracting herself from his hold, she paced across his office. The maneuver betrayed her, shouted her physical awareness of him, a fact that gave him an intense masculine satisfaction. It also roused the predator lurking within, filling him with the overwhelming urge to give chase.

She spun to face him. "You have no idea how difficult this is for me to say, and to you of all people. But I need your help."

"You have it."

Her chin trembled for a brief instant before she managed to firm it, anger coloring her words. "Could you find out who's doing this so I can stop them?"

He clamped down on the surge of relief. "I need to ask you a question first."

"Anything."

"How do you know that I'm not behind the incidents?"

Her anger drained away, leaving her eyes huge in a face gone stark-white. He heard the hitch to her breath and saw alarm bleed the vitality from her. "Oh God, Joc," she whispered. She took a swift step in his direction and lifted a hand in appeal. "Do you think I'm here because I suspect you?"

He was careful to keep his voice dispassionate. "Do

you? After all, I showed you who and what I am when I took down my partners at Deseos."

She dismissed that with a jerk of her shoulders. "You took down partners who were intent on stealing the island out from under you after you'd lent them a helping hand. I may not have known you for long, but it's been long enough to learn that you don't do business by burning barns or rustling cattle."

It was the oddest thing. It felt as though he'd been captured in a moment frozen by time. He could see Rosalyn staring up at him with total and utter faith. It seemed as though he had endless moments to search her expression, to look inward and assess the strength and veracity of that level of trust. To know that it existed. That she didn't have a single doubt about the honesty of his assertion. Just complete confidence and acceptance that his word was the absolute truth.

He couldn't take his eyes off her. Sunlight poured over her, setting her hair on fire around a face as pale and beautiful and compassionate as an angel's. "No one has ever trusted me." The words were ripped from him. "I've had to prove my honor again and again. Prove that I'm not the crook my father was."

A line formed between her brows. "I'm so sorry, Joc. That must have been difficult for you."

"No. You don't understand." He tried again. "You didn't demand proof that I wasn't involved. You didn't question my veracity. You accepted my word without a minute's hesitation or doubt."

"Oh." She thought about that for a second, before asking gravely, "Shouldn't I have?"

"Are you poking fun at me?" he asked in disbelief.

"Just a little bit." She pinched two fingers together. "A very little bit. You're sort of an easy target when it comes to that particular issue."

"Give me a straight answer, Red. Do you trust me, or not?"

She didn't hesitate this time, either. "Yes. I trust you."

"Now I have an even more important question for you." He decided to be as blunt as she'd been. "Are you pregnant?"

He knew the answer before she even opened her mouth, saw the mixture of wonder and nervousness that turned her eyes a brilliant shade of blue. "Yes, I'm pregnant. I found out right before the barn went up in flames."

As much as she trusted him, he still found it difficult to return the favor. "Were you going to tell me? If the barn hadn't burned, I mean?"

"Of course! This isn't something I'd keep from you. I promised."

There was no mistaking her sincerity. "Fair enough. I'll arrange for a doctor's visit as soon as we get to my place."

She held up her hands and took a swift step backward. "Whoa. Slow down, Arnaud. What do you mean...when we get to your place?"

"Do I have to spell it out for you, Red?" He crossed the room to confront her. "You're pregnant. Someone is destroying your property, and according to you it's escalating. It's not safe for you to stay at Longhorn." He invaded her space. "And just to be clear? This isn't open to negotiation."

She opened her mouth to argue. One look at his expression had her closing it again. After stewing for a few seconds, she asked, "What about my employees and animals? If I'm not safe, they aren't, either."

"I'll make arrangements to safeguard them all."

She brightened at that. "If you're going to safeguard my men and property, then there's no reason I can't return home."

"Only one."

"Which is?"

"I won't allow it."

Joc didn't give her an opportunity to come up with a response. Instead he did what he'd longed to since she'd first walked into his office and took her in his arms. His mouth locked over hers, the fit even more perfect than he remembered. She melted against him, as though their three-week separation had never been, responding with a fervent eagerness that made him wish they were back on Deseos with it's tropical breezes and sultry nights. Where a bed was only steps away and they were guaranteed endless days and nights of privacy to take their embrace to the ultimate conclusion. Instead he accepted what he could get in the here and now, and submerged himself in her unstinting warmth.

He knew this woman on a visceral level, recognized her scent and touch and taste. Most of all, he recognized the generosity with which she responded to him. He'd been a fool to think that a single night would satisfy either of them. He'd never be satisfied with just that one encounter. Not one embrace. Not one kiss. Not one night of lovemaking. What had started as a business encounter had become something reckless and passionate and infinitely dangerous. The softest of moans escaped as she opened to him, welcoming him home. Her hands crept beneath his suit jacket and splayed across his back, tugging him close. She sank into his kiss, her body moving helplessly against his.

He forked his hands into her hair and tilted her head so he'd have better access to her mouth. Then he drank, giving, taking, on the bare edge of control, showing her without words how much he'd missed her. A hunger filled him, a craving far worse than anything he'd experienced with any other woman. He wanted her. Here. Now. Any way he could have her. And even that wouldn't be enough. This craving was too intense to easily be sated. He might never have his fill of her or grow tired of having her in his arms.

She ended the kiss with unmistakable reluctance, snatching a final taste before pulling free. "That wasn't fair," she complained. She fought to bring some order to her hair and shirt. Glancing down, she groaned when she discovered that half her snaps had come undone. She fumbled to close them without much success. "And kissing me isn't going to make me forget our earlier discussion. You still haven't told me why I can't return to Longhorn if you're going to put safeguards in place. You can't just say you won't allow it and expect me to accept it."

"Then let me put it another way." He gathered her close and cupped her abdomen, warming her belly through the layers of denim and cotton. "I'll do anything and everything within my power to protect you and my child."

Seven

She shouldn't be surprised. She knew Joc was the take-charge type. So, finding herself bundled into his car and whisked off to the mansion he called a home shouldn't come as any surprise. What did surprise her was how he treated her in the next few days.

Initially he handled her as though she were made of fine crystal, as though the least word or touch risked shattering her. He didn't broach the subject of the baby, other than to arrange for a visit to the doctor so she could confirm both her pregnancy, as well as her overall health and well-being. She didn't expect his reticence to last long, not once he decided how he wanted to handle this latest development. Until then, he was playing his cards close to his chest.

As the days built toward a week, she discovered that

she didn't object to staying with Joc as much as she'd anticipated, though she did find what she privately dubbed his "quasi-palace" somewhat intimidating. It wasn't the size as much as the interior design. It struck her as uncomfortably formal, the pieces rich and elegant and reluctant to be touched. Not what she'd have called a home. As the first week passed and she became more integrated into his daily life, the differences between them became more and more apparent—and made her more and more uncomfortable.

How would she handle those differences now that she knew she was pregnant with his child? Would he expect their baby to live in his world? A frown touched her brow. How would that work? And of even greater concern, how did he expect her to fit in? The thought filled her with a panic that followed in her wake like an approaching storm front.

The guest rooms he offered for her use were the most sumptuous she'd ever seen. But she rattled around inside, lonely and uncomfortable while she waited to return to Longhorn. She'd spent most of the twenty-eight years of her life working from sunup until sundown. A life of leisure didn't suit her. Nor did feeling like she was a kept woman. She remained painfully aware that she wouldn't be here if it weren't for her pregnancy.

Joc's daily routine also caused problems. They met each morning at breakfast where an earnest young man would give Joc a report that encompassed everything from urgent news that had occurred during the night, to his schedule for the day, to calls, e-mails, and messages that could only be handled by the top man, himself.

Eventually Joc added another person to the mix—an earnest young woman who gave Rosalyn a similar report about the condition of her ranch, the investigation into the fire and other problems that had occurred on Longhorn since her return from Deseos. At the end of her first week with Joc, Rosalyn had had enough.

In the middle of the dual reports, she shoved back her chair. Picking up her plate and cup of coffee, she escaped the formal dining room for the lighter, friendlier sunroom that connected off the kitchen. It reminded her of the lanai on Deseos. Best of all, gentle morning light filled the spacious area and floor-to-ceiling windows offered a wide-ranging view of the garden. She deposited her breakfast and coffee on a small glass-and-wrought-iron café table and settled onto a thickly cushioned chair. She stretched, releasing a deep sigh of pleasure. Better. Much better.

"I gather you don't care for our morning briefing." Joc's voice came from the doorway behind her.

She didn't bother to turn around. "Not really."

"I thought it would help you to hear what efforts I'm making to find whoever's responsible for the problems at Longhorn. At least we know that it wasn't the men I fired for harassing you."

This time she did swivel to face him. "It does help to know that. Seriously, Joc. I appreciate everything you've done very much."

His mouth tugged to one side in a wry smile. "You just don't appreciate it over breakfast."

She shrugged. "I work every bit as hard as you—or I used to. But I don't spend every minute at it. And I surely don't allow it to interfere with my digestion."

His smile grew and he crossed to join her at the table. "We'll find the people responsible for your problems. I promise. In the meantime…" He dropped into the chair next to hers and took a swallow of the coffee he'd brought with him. "This is nice."

She sat quietly for several minutes while she polished off her breakfast. "As long as we're talking about changes to our routine, there's another one I'd like to make."

His voice took on a hard tone. "So long as it doesn't have anything to do with your return to Longhorn, you can have anything you want."

That had her eyebrows shooting upward. "You aren't going to ask what it is before you agree? That's not like you."

"Is this particular change open to negotiation?" A wicked gleam crept into his dark eyes. "I'm always happy to enter into a negotiation with you."

She shook her head. "Refuse and I'm out of here."

"That's what I figured." He leaned back in his chair and stretched out his long legs, hooking one ankle over the other. "Since that's the case, name it, Red, and it's yours," he offered expansively.

"Okay, fine. I don't like the bedroom you assigned me."

He frowned. "What's wrong with it? Whatever it is, I'll have it fixed by the end of day."

"Excellent." She took a final swallow of decaf coffee and shoved back her chair. "I'll move my stuff into your bedroom right away."

His cup crashed against the glass table. "What did you say?"

"You heard me." She met his gaze with as much composure as she could muster. "The baby's fine. I'm healthy. You don't have to treat me like I'll break. I thought after a few days, you'd get over it. But this is getting ridiculous."

He stared at her for an endless moment before exploding into action. One minute she was sitting at the table and the next he was propelling her through the mansion to his suite of rooms. The instant the door closed behind him, he wrapped his arms around her.

"Are you sure this is what you want?" he asked. "Be very certain, Red, because once I have you back in my bed, I'm not letting you out again."

"I'm positive."

Joc cupped her face and kissed her. With a low moan, she opened to him, holding nothing back. The bed rose up to meet her and he followed her down. The next few minutes passed in a breathless wrestling match as they both stripped off their clothes with frantic speed. When there was no more between them but heated flesh, they stilled, the encounter slowing, stretching, quieting as they cautiously opened one to the other.

Over the past few days Rosalyn had sat beneath the stars in Joc's formal garden and contemplated her feelings for him and for the baby he'd given her. Had looked up and absorbed some of the magic and mystery of those shards of hope sparkling above her. But in that moment, she realized there couldn't be a more magical or insightful moment than this.

Joc must have felt the same. With an incoherent exclamation, he lowered his head and kissed his way from her mouth to the beaded tips of breasts already showing the early changes her pregnancy wrought, to the still-flat expanse of her abdomen. And there he lingered, whispering a secret message to the child cradled deep beneath his lips.

Rosalyn closed her eyes against an unexpected wave of tears. She found this man endlessly fascinating, a creature of shadow and light, pain and grace. A hard man. A lonely man. A man who'd seen the worst and chosen to pursue the best. He offered their child its first kiss, explaining without words the emotions he fought so hard to deny. Each touch of his hand spoke of longing, of the need to connect, to belong. Didn't he see? Didn't he understand the importance of roots? Somehow, someway, she'd show him how vital they were. She slid her fingers deep into his hair and drew him to her, offering the only gift she could freely give.

Herself.

He came to her without words, finding his way home. Slipping between her thighs, he drove straight to the core of her with a single unerring stroke. She could feel the pain that filled him, that had haunted him for most of his life. She wrapped herself around him in response, absorbing the pain and replacing it with everything she had to give.

When she'd lost her family, she thought that feeling had been lost to her, as well. But she'd found it again. Found it within the arms of this man. With their joining, hope had returned.

And together, bound and tangled as one, they tumbled.

Hours later, Joc lifted onto an elbow and feathered a series of kisses from the curve of her jaw to the curve of her breast. "I have a charity gala toward the end of this month that I can't avoid." He lifted a shoulder in a half shrug. "Maybe that's because I'm the host. I'd appreciate it if you'd attend with me. And before you use the excuse that you have nothing to wear, I still have that beaded gown you wore on Deseos."

She started to refuse, but hesitated at the last moment, curiosity getting the better of her. "Why do you want me there?"

"Because I'd enjoy your company." He traced the path his mouth had taken with his fingertips, eliciting a helpless shiver. "I won't even try to negotiate with you about it. It's a no-strings-attached invitation."

"I wouldn't fit in," she demurred.

"Your family is one of the oldest in Texas." There was a vague brusqueness underscoring his comment, one she didn't comprehend until he added, "Trust me, you fit in better than I do."

"Oh." She caught her lower lip between her teeth as a possibility occurred to her. The Hollister name was also one of the oldest in Texas. "Will they be there?"

He didn't pretend to misunderstand. "Probably. My Hollister relatives attend most of the local charitable affairs. Since I'm hosting the event, we may get lucky and be spared their presence."

"How do they react when you all meet?"

"It depends on what they need from me. It runs the gamut from smoldering glares to demands for excessive donations to looking at me as though I were something unpleasant they'd accidentally stepped in."

That simple explanation said so much, revealed so much of what he'd gone through over the years. Her heart went out to him. "I'm sorry."

"Don't let it bother you. I don't."

Did he really believe that? Or was that how he managed to get past the pain they inflicted? She couldn't bear the idea of him facing MacKenzie on his own, not after what she'd pulled with Joc's partners on Deseos. "Yes, I'll go with you."

He traced a delicious circle around the tip of her breast. "A pity date, Red?"

She shivered beneath the teasing caress. "You think I pity the great Joc Arnaud?" she managed to scoff. "Not even a little. Besides…" She slanted him a teasing look. "Do you want to see me in that beaded dress again or not?"

"Hell, yes."

"Then where's the problem?"

"The problem is that I'm going to want to strip you out of that dress as soon as I see you in it." His voice dropped to a husky whisper, one filled with tender amusement. "But at least now I know that you're going to let me."

"So, what's the point of tonight's affair?" she asked several weeks later on the drive to the gala. "Or is there a point?"

"Charity. We're raising funds for the National Marrow Donor Program."

"Excellent. I hope you're also twisting a few arms so that people do more than contribute money. Let's hope they also join the registry."

His smile flashed white in the darkness. "That's why I find you so fascinating, Red. You don't care about the odds. You're always on your feet, ready to battle for the underdog."

"I have to admit, right now I feel like one of those underdogs." At his quizzical glance, she clarified, "I'm a bit out of my element this evening."

"You'll get used to it."

She shot him a look of alarm. "What does that mean?"

"Just what I said. In time, you'll get used to these black-tie events and it won't bother you anymore."

She shifted in her seat to face him. "Listen to me, Joc. I have no intention of getting used to this or any other part of your lifestyle. I don't belong here. I belong on a ranch, dressed in a pair of jeans that are so old and worn that they know to wrap themselves around a horse's belly without even being asked. I don't belong in this latest getup that makes me feel like I'm…I'm—"

She couldn't bring herself to say "a kept woman," which might be just as well considering the way Joc tensed. He didn't say a word, which made her all the more apprehensive. Shadows burrowed into the rough-cut angles of his face, making his appearance more austere than usual. Only his eyes glittered, the color as black and hard as obsidian.

"You will tell me if anyone so much as suggests such a thing about you."

"And you'll do what?" she asked, genuinely curious. "Give them hell? Threaten them? Destroy them for daring to speak the truth?"

She struggled to ignore his crisp, masculine scent, to forget how protected she felt when he held her in those powerful arms. Or how delicate and feminine she was when he swept her against the hard, broad expanse of his chest. But how could she? From the moment they'd met they'd been unable to keep their hands off each other. And from that desire, a desire unlike anything she'd ever experienced before, a miracle had been created. She struggled to gather up her emotions so that she could continue without betraying her inner turmoil.

"Don't you get it? I walked into our relationship with my eyes wide-open. I wanted to sleep with you, to cut loose for once in my life. So, I did. But it came with consequences, and I'll pay the price. But don't expect me to be happy about it."

He stiffened. "You consider our baby a price you have to pay?" The question cracked like a whip. "Is that how you think of him?"

Her breath caught in dismay. "No, of course not. I didn't mean the baby, I meant tonight. Being in this getup is the price I have to pay."

He seemed torn between laughter and anger. "Most women wouldn't consider tonight some sort of punishment."

"Yeah, well. I'm not most women," she muttered.

"No, you're not." He reached for her and drew his thumb along the curve of her cheek to her mouth, tracing the full sweep of her lower lip. "I don't want you to be anyone other than yourself. I've had my fill of women trying to conform themselves to my expectations. Or to what they perceive as my expectations. I'm not interested in them. I'm interested in you."

"For the sake of my ranch. For the sake of the child I'm carrying."

"I'm interested in you because of what you do to me anytime I come near you. I thought that one night would take care of it. But it hasn't. Nor have the past several weeks, or what we were doing right before we left the house. If anything, I want you more than ever."

"It won't work, Joc. We come from different worlds, with too many issues between us to think anything can come out of whatever this is between us. My priorities have to be my baby and my ranch—a ranch you're still thinking of taking from me."

The limo drew to a halt just then and light poured into the back, cutting across his face with sharp precision. What she saw revealed there had her catching her breath in dismay. She'd hurt him. She wouldn't have thought it possible. But for that one instant, she saw the wound that blanked his eyes and spasmed across his expression.

"Joc—"

He cut her off without compunction. "Don't. I know on an intellectual level you don't trust me because I still intend to purchase Longhorn."

"I do trust you."

He shook his head. "Not yet. Not completely. Not when it comes to our baby or your ranch. But there have been other occasions when you haven't had time to think, when you've had to go with your gut instinct. Those are the times that count. Because each and every one of those times, you've trusted me. You went with me to Deseos. You allowed me to make love to you. You believed me when I said I wasn't responsible for the problems on your ranch. You've believed me based on no more than my word, alone." He tilted his head to one side. "Have you ever wondered why?"

And with that he exited the limousine, leaving her to

sit in stunned silence. It was an excellent question. It was also one she didn't dare answer...because that answer threatened to tear her world apart.

From the moment they entered the charity gala, Joc played the role of gallant escort and affable patron to the hilt. No one was more charming. Or gracious. Or witty.

Rosalyn watched his performance with growing dismay. She hadn't realized until that moment how completely Joc had let down his guard around her. She didn't know this man, though she suspected most everyone else here did. Worse, she disliked this caricature of the man she loved with tear-provoking intensity. They were emotions wrought from hormonal imbalance, she tried to tell herself, partially from the baby and partially from having surrendered to her need to be with Joc. But deep down she recognized the lie for what it was.

With every ounce of passion she possessed, she longed for the man who'd swept her off to Deseos. And she accepted the fact that she'd helped nail in place the facade he now wielded with such skill. She wanted her wolf back. Elemental. Keen-eyed. Ruthless.

Loving.

Rosalyn found herself so focused on Joc and how he'd changed that she didn't at first notice people's reaction to her. She was surprised to discover that those Joc introduced her to were friendly, for the most part, though she couldn't have said why she expected anything different. Some were speculative, and a select few were assessing, as though seeing a new playing piece on a game board and wondering how best to maneuver it to their advantage. Well, they'd soon discover that her particular game piece wielded no power and held no advantage. Maybe she should make it easy for them and stamp Pawn across her forehead.

Halfway through the evening, she realized she was actually having a good time. At least she was right up until a woman approached them, a woman who could have passed for Joc's twin. Familiar deep-set black eyes glittered within a striking face accentuated by high, elegant cheekbones and a wide, sensuous mouth—a mouth curved into a cold smile.

Joc inclined his head. "MacKenzie," he greeted the woman, confirming her identity. "Hope you're enjoying the gala. I believe the buffet table has a generous helping of sour grapes I ordered for your personal enjoyment."

"You think you won?" She laughed. "Deseos was just my first volley in our little war."

"A volley you lost."

Her amusement faded and she shrugged. "True. But I won't lose the next round. Of course, if you sell the Hollister homestead to me, there won't be another round."

He shook his head before she'd even finished speaking. "That's not going to happen, MacKenzie. You couldn't afford it even if I were willing to sell."

Anger glittered in her dark eyes. "What did you do to her all those years ago?" she demanded in a low voice. "How did you manage to steal that property away from my mother? What hold do you have over her that she neglected to tell us she sold our home to you a full decade ago? Tell me, Joc! What dirty little secret did you uncover that forced her to sell out to you?"

He simply shook his head, his expression giving nothing away. "I suggest you ask your mother those questions."

She balled her hands into fists, frustration implicit in every line of her body. "I have. She won't tell me. I've been asking ever since I found out—a full year ago."

"Because there's nothing to tell." He made the comment with surprising gentleness. "Maybe the land holds bad memories for her. It would be understandable, all things considered. Boss's activities couldn't have been easy for Meredith, any more than they were for the rest of us."

She cut him off with a swipe of her hand. "I don't want your pity. Just because you've made it big by swindling widows out of their life's savings doesn't mean that people actually respect or like you. They just want your money. Or didn't that little incident on Deseos prove how little regard your friends have for you?" Her gaze shifted to Rosalyn and narrowed. "You're making a mistake being with him. You will regret it, I promise."

"Don't." Joc's voice cut sharper than she'd ever heard it. "You want to come after me, fine. But you leave Rosalyn out of it."

"If you don't want her in the line of fire, don't put her there." With that MacKenzie turned on her designer-clad heel and stalked away.

Joc immediately grasped Rosalyn's hand and swung her onto the dance floor. "Relax. You don't want her to see that she got to you."

"I don't have the practice you do at concealing my feelings." She did her best to smooth the signs of distress from her face. "Just out of curiosity... Why won't you sell the Hollister homestead to her?"

"She can't afford it, for one thing."

Rosalyn shot him a sharp look. "Don't lie to me, Joc. If you don't want to tell me, fine. But it's not the money that's stopping you. If you wanted her to have the property, you'd be generous enough to price it at something she can afford." When he didn't reply, she tried again. "You know, holding on to the Hollister homestead is inconsistent with what you told me about your attitude toward family and connections. Are you sure this particular land isn't more than mere dirt to you? Maybe you don't want to sell because it gives you a connection with your own roots."

"It's an interesting theory, but wrong." His hand left her waist to cup her chin and force her to look at him. "Let's make a pact, you and I."

She tensed within his hold and stared up at him with undisguised wariness. "What sort of pact?"

"For the next ten minutes let's agree that everything we say to each other will be the absolute, dead-honest truth. Agreed?" At her nod, he said, "I despise what my father did to all of us. The Hollisters. My mother. My sister and me. I won't go into the reasons I bought the land, but trust me. It has nothing whatsoever to do with unresolved daddy issues."

"Then what?"

"No way, Red. Now it's my turn." His pinned her in place as they drifted across the dance floor. "First question. When you walked into the conference room, you were attracted to me, weren't you?"

Okay, she could answer that one with reasonable honesty. "Yes, I was attracted to you, which confused me no end."

"I can imagine."

The corner of her mouth kicked upward. "I was furious at you for siccing your goons on me. I actually hated you for your unremitting attempts to try to force me to sell my ranch. And I assumed that hate would grow by leaps and bounds when I confronted you in the boardroom." Her smile turned bittersweet. What a fool she'd been. "It didn't."

Held within his arms, she could feel his gathering tension. "You're joking."

"No." The admission came hard, almost as hard as when she'd first realized the truth. "It's not something I'm happy about, you understand."

"I can imagine." He waited a beat, before pressing on. "And when we shook hands? Do you remember that?"

Rosalyn froze. She understood then, understood his plan and what he hoped to accomplish with his questions. He wanted her to remember. Remember how she'd responded to him. Felt. Ached. Hungered. He wanted her to confront the truth head-on and experience those same reactions all over again. She wanted to lie. Badly. But she'd agreed to answer his question truthfully, and come hell or high water, she would—even if doing so stripped a few protective layers off her hide.

A combination of pain and regret washed through her. "I wish I could forget that moment." More, she wished it hadn't changed something vital inside her—all because Joc had come into her world and turned it upside down.

"But you can't, any more than I can."

When she didn't respond right away, his hand drifted from her face to her shoulders, generating a path of fire. The song ended and he urged her from the dance floor and through a bank of doors that opened onto a huge garden. Dusk had settled in and the heady scent of evening primroses heralded the approach of night. Soft lighting illuminated the pathways, allowing them to wander at will.

"You haven't answered me, Red," Joc prompted. "What did you feel when we first touched?"

Her movements slowed as they followed one of the deserted walkways. What she'd felt then was no different from how she felt now. "It was just a casual contact," she whispered. "Two strangers shaking hands."

"But it generated instant heat."

"Made an instant connection." She paused in a small alcove formed by a stand of lilacs and closed her eyes in a vain attempt to block him out. To her distress, it only intensified her awareness, sharpening her other senses. Heaven help her, but she wanted him. "I was attracted to you," she admitted. "More attracted than I've ever been to anyone before."

The words hung in the air for an endless second. Joc pulled her closer, mating their bodies, locking them together in a fit that could only be described as sheer perfection. "And when we were at Longhorn? When I brushed the hair out of your eyes. Do you remember how you reacted to me then?"

She clamped her teeth together and turned her head away. "What does it matter?"

"Did you feel it? Did you feel the heat? The connection?"

"Of course I felt it." She opened her eyes, her gaze drawn to him like a moth to flame. "It was all hot connection and broken circuits with a bit of lust thrown in for good measure."

"That's how strong the chemistry was before that night on Deseos. Before we made love. How it's been from the start. Nothing has changed, has it? In fact, it's only grown stronger. Every time we touch. Every time we kiss. From the moment we made love. It caused whatever this is between us to become more powerful. Isn't that the truth?"

"Yes, it's true." And the truth made her want to weep. "I can't keep my hands off you. I don't want to keep my hands off you."

She couldn't resist looking at him again. And that was all it took. It happened again, just like the first time. The instant heat, the desperate want, the sizzle and burn that came whenever they were within touching distance. He must have read the admission on her face, felt it in the helpless give of her body, because he acknowledged it with a knowing smile.

And then he kissed her. She'd anticipated a kiss of possession, a hard and passionate storming, designed to breach her defenses. And it did breach them, just not through strength. He slipped beneath her guard with a gentle taking, the passion a light, joyous exchange. Worse, he offered no more than a prelude, a reminder of how it had been and what it could become once more. He tantalized her with a single taste before setting her free. But that one taste wasn't enough. Could never be enough. All it did was intensify the craving without offering any satisfaction.

"Why are you doing this?" she asked unsteadily. "What do you want?"

"You're pregnant with my baby, Red. I want you to marry me."

Eight

"She turned me down flat, Ana." Joc paced his study, as he waited impatiently for his sister's response.

"Let me guess. You proposed a business merger instead of a marriage."

"I'm not that stupid," he retorted, stung.

"Oh, really? This is Joc Arnaud, right?" She tapped the receiver with her fingernail. "Hello? Hello? Who are you, and what have you done with my big brother?"

"Damn it, Ana—"

She cut him off without compunction. "No way, Joc. You don't get off that easily. Allow me to refresh your memory, brother dear. Are you, or are you not the same man who signed a contract with Prince Lander Montgomery and made marriage to me a clause in said contract?"

"Rosalyn's pregnant with my child."

Dead silence greeted his statement. "I'd ask how that happened," she said at length, "but I'm forced to assume it was in the usual way. I'm surprised. Check that. I'm not surprised, I'm flat-out shocked. You're normally so scrupulous about those things."

He spoke between clenched teeth. "Could we stay on topic? It happened. Now she won't marry me."

"I don't suppose you proposed to her once you found out she was pregnant?"

"Of course I did. What other choice was there?"

"Oh, Joc. For such a brilliant man, there are times you can be as thick and brainless as the proverbial brick. Hang on a sec. Lander just walked in." A brief, muffled conversation followed, and then Ana came back on the line. "My husband wants me to give you a message."

Joc thrust a hand through his hair. "Hell."

"He said he warned you that one day you'd find yourself boxed into the sort of corner you boxed him in. And that you were supposed to remember him when that day came." Her tone grew dry. "I think that's Verdonian for 'I told you so.'"

"I called you for advice, Ana," Joc snarled. "Not so you and Prince Not-So-Charming could rub my nose in my mistakes."

"Fine. Here's my advice. Women want to be married for love. It's that simple."

He opened his mouth and closed it again. Love. Damn. Why did it have to be love? He could negotiate his way around any number of troublesome issues. But not that one. He drew the line at making claims he couldn't back up with hard evidence, especially not when it came to something that serious. He cared for Rosalyn. He wanted her with a passion that defied understanding. But love? He shook his head. He'd never trust a woman that far or expose himself to that sort of vulnerability.

"There must be an alternative. What other choices do I have?" he demanded.

"Well, you can always follow in Lander's footsteps and simply announce your engagement to the press. But I wouldn't recommend it. I doubt Rosalyn will take it any better than I did."

"Thanks, Ana. I'll think about it."

"So, when's the baby due?"

"Mid-February," he replied absently.

Maybe if he offered to end his negotiations to buy Longhorn she'd reconsider his proposal. With any other person, that would undoubtedly work. Any other person would be downright grateful. But somehow he had the feeling that gratitude would be way down on the list of Rosalyn's reactions. Like, maybe dead last.

"That's fantastic," Ana was saying. "The two cousins will share a birthday."

It took a minute for that to sink in. Once it had, it stopped him dead in his tracks. "*What?* Ana, are you pregnant?"

"Wow. Score one for the financial genius," she said with a laugh. "Maybe you aren't so brainless, after all. I'll talk to you later, Joc. Good luck with Rosalyn. Let me know what happens." And with that she cut the connection.

Joc tossed the phone aside and leaned against the desk in his study. He scrubbed his hands across his face.

There had to be a way around his predicament. Something that Rosalyn wanted enough to agree to marriage. Analyzing the problem from a business standpoint filled him with a calm determination. He just had to find the right lever that would win her agreement. Because he wouldn't claim to love her when he didn't. And he sure as hell didn't love her. That decided, he went to find his woman and start the negotiations.

It was well past midnight before Rosalyn slipped into the room she shared with Joc. The instant they arrived home from the charity gala, she raided the kitchen, desperate for a light snack, while Joc excused himself to make a phone call. She didn't know how long he'd be, but she suspected he would want to return to the subject of marriage, something she'd managed to avoid during those final few hours of the night's affair. She'd seen it in the determination burning in his gaze each time he looked at her, as well as the hard set of his mouth.

Tension built across her shoulders at the thought of another confrontation. More than anything she wanted to strip away her evening finery and crawl into something plain and comfortable and, above all else, cotton. Somehow she didn't think she owned any cotton anymore, and probably wouldn't as long as she lived under Joc's roof. Kicking off her heels, she reached behind her to ease down the zip. Her fingers collided with Joc's.

"Let me help," he murmured.

Her heart picked up a beat. "I didn't hear you come in."

"No, you were lost in thought."

He helped her strip off the gown, along with the ridiculous thong, before dropping a nightgown over her head that felt remarkably like cotton. She gathered it up, her tension draining away. "It *is* cotton," she said in delight. "Where did this come from?"

"From me. I noticed over the past few weeks that you weren't comfortable wearing the other nightgowns I purchased for you."

She shrugged awkwardly. "They were all silk and I'm used to something a bit plainer." She ran her hand over the fabric, realizing as she did so that the cotton she wore at home held little similarity to what was clearly an Egyptian blend with a thread count in the trillions. It amazed her what such a small change made to her overall well-being. It felt good to be back to normal. Or almost normal. "Thank you."

He crossed the room, stripping off his tux as he went. She eyed him apprehensively. They were interrupted right after she'd refused his proposal and there hadn't been an opportunity to discuss it further. She suspected that wouldn't be the case for much longer and she had to admit, she didn't have a clue how to handle the conversation.

Giving herself time to think, she bent her head and spread her hand low across her abdomen, marveling that a life grew there. Dear God, a baby. She still hadn't absorbed the full meaning of the event. A moment later, Joc crouched in front of her, his hand joining hers over the life growing in her womb.

"We need to protect this little one," he said.

His simple statement had her slipping from his grasp and retreating across the room. She gathered the last remaining vestiges of her fading energy. Time to deal with his proposal once and for all. "And marriage will do that?"

"You had to know this particular negotiation was coming." He pursued her, his intonation remaining calm and cool. Painfully businesslike. "You had to at least suspect that I wouldn't allow a child of mine to come into this world a bastard. Been there, done that. And it's not happening to my baby."

"He or she will be an Oakley, not a bastard. And that's not open to negotiation."

He'd boxed her in so she couldn't retreat any farther. "Wrong, Red. He's going to be an Arnaud. I won't compromise on that point. I'm willing to make concessions on any other stipulations you'd care to name. But not that one." His face settled into inflexible lines. "I told you about my childhood. I told you how my sister and I suffered. Are you willing to inflict that on our baby?"

"What I'll be inflicting on our baby is Oakley roots," she corrected. "The Oakley line will continue. This isn't the way I planned to do it, but since it's happened and there's no changing it, I want our child to sink his roots as deeply into Texan soil as I have. Those roots may mean nothing to you, but they mean everything to me."

"Don't you get it?" The question held an edge of impatience. "His roots may be planted in your world, but he'll have to live in mine."

She released her breath in a rough sigh. "Face facts, Joc. I don't fit in your world. I'll never fit in your world."

"You will. And so will our child."

How could he say that? "Because you say so?"

"Yes."

Simple and direct. She groaned. And probably true. When Joc Arnaud spoke, everyone else jumped. Well, not her. "Look—"

He cut her off. "No, you look. This baby will be under a microscope from the minute he's born. I will do whatever necessary to protect him from that onslaught, to raise him—" He broke off and lowered his head, reminding her of a wounded animal gathering himself for a final, desperate attack. "To raise him with honor and integrity and...and love."

"Oh, Joc," she whispered.

"Listen to me, Red." A hint of strain colored his words, as though he were fighting a pitched battle. And maybe he was. It occurred to her that this was probably the most important negotiation of his life. "We can make this work. I know we can. There's something there between us. Something that binds us. Something more than the baby."

She fought to keep every scrap of hope from her voice. "Are you saying you love me?"

"I don't know how to love. That's the God's honest truth." His jaw worked for a moment. "But I'm willing to try."

"Marrying you won't change my need for roots. Having your baby won't either. If anything it sends those roots that much deeper." Unable to help herself, she cupped his face in her hands. "You have to know what you're letting yourself in for."

"I have a fair idea."

She shook her head. "It isn't just me, Joc. You'll also have to deal with those roots you dread. That connection

you deny. Our son or daughter will grow strong and tall."
She feathered a kiss across his mouth, encouraged by his
instant response, a response that came without hesitation
or forethought. "And it will be at Longhorn. That's where
he or she will learn to appreciate the land and the importance of emotional integrity over materialistic excess. I
want my child raised there, not out of some corporate
headquarters or quasi-palace. And if they are raised there,
they'll put down more roots, roots you won't be able to
yank free any more than you could mine."

"And if I don't agree?"

"Then I won't marry you and there's nothing you can
do to force me into it." She released him and stepped
away, allowing cool air to replace the warmth of her
embrace. An odd smile tugged at the corners of her
mouth. "For some reason I've been having these bizarre
dreams about trees. I don't know, maybe it's the change
in hormones. Whatever the cause, it made me realize
something. Some trees can't reproduce without being
grafted, one onto another."

He tilted his head to one side, considering. "Is that what
we've done, Red? Have we grafted onto each other?"

Her smile grew. "I haven't heard what we were doing
that night on Deseos described quite that way before.
But however you want to put it, the graft took. Our tree
is definitely reproducing."

"True enough." He gave her offer some serious
thought. "I'm beginning to understand why Hades
forced Persephone to live in the Underworld with him
each winter. At least that way he had her in his world
for part of each year."

"Is that what you want to negotiate next? You want me to play Persephone to your Hades?"

He shook his head. "I couldn't do that." He dropped his head and considered for a moment. "If I agree that our son or daughter—all of our sons and daughters—will be raised at Longhorn, will you marry me?"

Tears filled her eyes. "Yes, Joc. I'll marry you. And I'm hoping, really hoping, that Longhorn will be as much your home as it's been mine."

"Then we have an agreement."

She released her breath in an exasperated sigh. "Why do I feel as though we should be shaking hands?"

"There's only one way to seal a bargain with you." He approached, his movements filled with a lazy grace. He slid his hand beneath her hair along her nape and eased her up to meet his kiss. He took his time, the kiss slow and thorough and filled with unmistakable hunger. When he finally released her, he said, "There's a seventy-two-hour waiting period before we can marry. Or we can fly to Vegas and get it done in the morning."

She continued to stare at him, trying to see past the barriers straight to his heart and soul. "You and I, we're Texans, Joc. This is where we should marry."

He nodded in agreement. "What do you say we apply for that license first thing in the morning?"

"I'd like that."

His voice lowered, roughened. "I swear I won't let you down."

And that was all it took. She fell into his arms and allowed herself to believe, to believe that somehow it would all work out and that this marriage they contemplated had a real shot at success. To believe that one day he'd fall in love with her.

Because somehow, at some point, Little Red Riding Hood had fallen in love with the Big, Bad Wolf.

Perhaps it was the silence that woke him, that hushed moment where night gave over to day. That particular instant when the creatures that serenaded the night fell silent and those that welcomed the day slept. Or maybe it was the absolute rightness of having Rosalyn back in his arms, tucked so close that Joc couldn't distinguish between her heartbeat and his own.

He'd never before experienced such contentment. Never known such pleasure and satisfaction. It was the baby, he tried to tell himself. That explained the connection he felt to Rosalyn. She was pregnant and he was the man responsible. He'd have felt the same no matter who carried his child.

An image of other women and other occasions flickered in and out of his head, offering a swift reminiscence of time and place and romantic encounter. And one by one he dismissed them, dismissed them all without so much as a moment's hesitation. They were wrong, each and every one of them. Worse, it felt wrong thinking about them with Rosalyn sound asleep in his arms.

The time had come to face facts.

This woman was different. He'd known it from the moment he'd first set eyes on her. Everything within him urged him to take her. To keep her. To protect her with every ounce of power, money and skill at his disposal.

He closed his eyes, facing the unpalatable truth. And even that wouldn't be sufficient. Rosalyn didn't want his power or his money or his skill. She only wanted one thing, whether she recognized the truth or not. She wanted his heart—a heart he wasn't sure he possessed.

Because loving meant trusting. Loving meant surrender. Loving meant loss, or the risk of loss. It was fine to demand those things from others so long as he remained protected from the threat they posed. How long had he worked to ensure just that? A lifetime. Somehow Rosalyn had changed all that. She'd stormed into his life and altered him in some indelible way. He couldn't go back to the man he was. Nor could he allow this current opportunity to slip away.

"Joc?"

He smiled at the way his name escaped her throat—half moan, or was it more of a groan? "I'm here, Red."

Her eyes remained shut, her voice faint and wistful. "I had a dream. We planted the most incredible tree, the biggest tree in the entire world. And it grew into a giant forest filled with all these magical creatures. I wish we could go there."

He brushed her mouth with a kiss. "Did I help you plant the tree?"

"Of course. Joc?"

"I'm still here."

"Let's go plant a tree tomorrow."

He closed his eyes, filled with a contentment unlike any he'd felt before. "I'd like that."

Even more he'd like to be around to watch it grow and

spread its branches, to fill up the sky and seed an entire forest. Somehow that appealed far more than any project currently resting on his desk. For that matter, it appealed far more than any project that had ever crossed his desk.

And in that hushed moment where night gave over to day, that peculiar instant when the creatures that serenaded the night fell silent and those that welcomed the day slept, Joc surrendered to the inevitable. His hand slipped around her waist and cupped his future, warming it within his palm.

No, not his future. Their future.

They woke the next morning to disaster. A call from Claire had them driving out to Longhorn as quickly as the speed limit allowed. Off in the distance, rain-laden thunderheads piled up, tumbling closer with each mile they covered.

"I don't understand," Rosalyn fussed. "Why wouldn't she tell us what's wrong?"

"She'll explain when we get there," Joc tried to assure her.

Rosalyn felt the color bleed from her face. "There's been another fire. Someone's burned down the ranch house."

"We wouldn't be meeting Claire there if that were the case. Stay calm, Red. Whatever it is, we'll deal with it. Together."

And with that, she had to be satisfied. To her relief, the homestead still stood, and her heart quickened at the sight. Until they'd pulled into the long, gravel driveway, she hadn't realized how much she missed being home.

She could see Claire standing on the porch, tension vibrating off her motherly frame.

Rosalyn jumped out of the car the instant Joc pulled to a stop. "What's the problem?" she demanded.

"I'll give it to you straight. Some townie sashayed in here and insisted to see you. I tried to run her off, but she wouldn't budge. Said she'd wait until you got home. Rosalyn…" Claire twisted her hands together. "She's claiming she owns the place."

"What?" Rosalyn tried to laugh, but for some reason her throat had gone bone-dry. She shoved open the front door and stepped into the foyer, just as the skies opened. Rain slapped against the glass panels on either side of the front door with an urgent staccato. "Where is she?"

"I put her in the living room."

Joc stepped forward. "Red—"

She spun to confront him. "Do you know anything about this?"

There was a long, hideous pause. Then he asked, "Are you asking if I've somehow found a way to steal your ranch from you?"

She should have been warned by the extreme calm with which he spoke, or the way his eyes went flat and cold. But suspicion had taken hold and nothing would shake it. "Have you found a way?"

"So much for trust."

She could hear a small voice, deep inside, screaming at her to take the words back. But another voice, just as insistent, reminded her that Joc was the sort of man who wanted it all—her, their child and her ranch. And if an opportunity presented itself to seize control and gain leverage over the situation, he'd take it. Especially if it gave him everything he wanted.

"Let's find out what's going on," she said, ignoring his comment.

She turned on her heel and hastened down the flagstone steps into the living room. She caught her first glimpse of their visitor and nearly gasped in shock. Behind her, she heard Joc swear. Then, "MacKenzie, what the hell are you doing here?"

"I'm checking out my latest acquisition." She leaned back in the chair she'd commandeered and crossed her legs. "What are you doing here, brother dear?"

The wind kicked up, rattling the shutters while the rain began clawing at the windowpanes. "I belong here, which is more than I can say for you."

"Not anymore. You and your…" She lifted an eyebrow. "Friend?"

"Fiancée."

MacKenzie laughed. "That's rich."

"Stop it, both of you!" Rosalyn burst out. "I want to know what's going on."

MacKenzie swung her foot back and forth in a leisurely rhythm. "It's really very simple. You're a pawn, my dear. My brother wanted your land, which means so do I. In the normal course of things, he'd have found a business angle to use in order to get it. I would have then countered. And in the end, one of us would have won and the other lost." She glanced in Joc's direction. "Isn't that how the game's played?"

"This isn't a game," he answered.

"Of course it is. You've just changed the rules a bit.

Instead of paying for your pleasure, you've decided to romance it away from the poor, gullible rancher." MacKenzie switched her gaze back to Rosalyn. "That's you, in case you didn't realize. Only, he's too late. As soon as I learned he wanted this property, I purchased the note. I then made…oh, let's call them certain arrangements with a gentleman named Duff. Did you know your ranch hand has a gambling problem?"

Beside her Joc swore and Rosalyn fought to speak without her voice trembling. "You bribed him?"

MacKenzie lifted a shoulder in a casual shrug. "I can't be held responsible if your employee kept forgetting to mail the mortgage. Nor can I be held responsible if you never caught the omission. A piece of advice. You really should balance your bank accounts more often. I'd have thought Joc would have taught you that much, if nothing else."

Rosalyn shook her head. "No. That can't be right."

"It's right." A hint of sympathy touched the other woman's face. "You'll find that when it comes to cutthroat business deals, I'm as good as my brother."

"What do you want, MacKenzie?" Joc broke in.

She offered him a sunny smile. "Not a thing. I have what I came for. You're just annoyed because I got here ahead of you and managed to block whatever development deal you have going. I guess that land you purchased all around the Oakley place was a waste of good money." She tisked in mock sympathy. "What a shame."

"This has nothing to do with Rosalyn. Don't put her in the middle."

"I didn't. You did," his sister shot back. "I warned

you about that last night, but as usual the all powerful Joc Arnaud thought he held the winning cards. Well, you don't."

"You're the one who's caused all the problems around here," Rosalyn accused. "The one who burned down my barn."

MacKenzie frowned. "I most certainly did not. I merely asked Duff to keep you busy so you wouldn't have time to realize I was foreclosing on you. I can't be responsible if he was a trifle overzealous."

Rosalyn's hands balled into fists. "You're treating this like it's some sort of game. Or a joke. It's not! This is my life. This is my home."

"Not anymore." MacKenzie swept to her feet. "You have until the end of the week to clear out."

"MacKenzie," Joc growled. "Don't do this. She's an innocent bystander in our little feud."

A cold, bitter anger settled over his half sister's features. Overhead thunder boomed as the storm closed in. "Allow me to make myself clear to both of you. Nothing you say or do will change my mind."

Rosalyn drop-kicked her pride. "I'll make up the payments," she pleaded.

Joc dropped a heavy hand on her shoulder. "Red—"

She shook him off and continued to address Mac-Kenzie. "I have the money. I'll pay whatever penalty you require. I should have balanced my accounts, I admit that. Please don't take my home."

"I suggest if you want to blame someone for this mess, blame Joc. He's the one who refuses to sell me the Hollister homestead." She collected her purse and crossed to the steps leading to the hallway. "Just so we're clear, I won't be changing my mind. I suggest you start packing. Because if you're not out by the end of the week, I'll send the law out here to forcibly remove you. First thing Monday morning I'm bringing in the bulldozers and I intend to raze every last structure on this land."

Rosalyn fought to breathe. No. She couldn't mean it. She looked at Joc and that's when she knew. Not only did MacKenzie mean it, but she intended to do it. And there wasn't a chance in the world that Joc or anyone else could stop her.

Without a word, Rosalyn shoved past MacKenzie, intent on escape. She raced up the steps and hit the loosened carpet just outside the living room at a dead-run. Too late she remembered that she'd never had it tacked down. She hooked it with her boot heel and started to trip. She pinwheeled in a desperate effort to save herself. For a split second, she thought she'd be able to, that her foolishness wouldn't meet with disaster. But then she pitched backward toward the stairs. Two thoughts haunted her in those few precious seconds before she hit.

She'd never told Joc she loved him.

But far worse, her thoughtlessness had killed her baby.

Nine

"Red? Oh God. Talk to me, Red."

Joc dropped to her side and carefully lifted the side-board that had tipped onto her when she'd clipped it falling down the steps. She didn't move. Yanking out his cell phone, he placed an emergency call. The connection phased in and out because of the storm, making it difficult for him to relay the necessary information. It soon became clear that it would be impossible to send in a Life Flight helicopter given the current weather conditions.

During the endless minutes that followed, she didn't stir. More frightened than he could ever remember being, he checked for a pulse. When he found it, he could have bawled like a baby. He spared MacKenzie a deadly glare. "Get out," he ordered. He didn't bother watching to see if she obeyed, instead returning to the call. Demanding. Pleading. Swearing.

The next half hour, as he waited for the EMTs to arrive, proved the longest of his life, driving him to the very brink of despair. If Claire hadn't been there, her steady, reassuring voice a comforting balm, he'd have totally lost it. He crouched above Rosalyn, more helpless than he'd ever been before in his life. The great Joc Arnaud couldn't buy or bargain or bribe his way out of this disaster. There was only one thing he could do, something he didn't remember ever having tried before.

He prayed.

Once the emergency personnel arrived, they stabilized Rosalyn before whisking her out to the ambulance. He lost count of the number of times he told them she was pregnant. Or how many times he told them they were supposed to marry in less than seventy-two hours. He offered everything he could think of in exchange for their help in saving her. None of it did any good. The events of that night leaked through his fingers on a course all their own, beyond his ability to direct or control.

It wasn't until the paramedics had loaded Rosalyn into the ambulance that he faced a truth he'd been dodging for weeks. He loved her. He loved her more than life itself. How could he have not recognized it sooner? Maybe because he'd never experienced such depth of emotion before, not that it mattered now. During the endless ride to the hospital, he made up for that lapse. He didn't know whether she heard. He could only hope that somehow, someway, his words slipped through to that realm of oblivion where she hid from him.

He'd been blind not to have recognized his feelings sooner, to have believed that what he felt for her could be anything less than love. The first chance he got, he'd correct that oversight. He just needed one more chance. That was all. Just one.

He couldn't disguise his relief when they arrived at the hospital. He glanced down at Rosalyn. She lay on a bed of white, her skin and face almost as pale. Only her flame-bright hair provided any color. He took her hand in his as they barreled through the ER doors. It didn't occur to him that he wouldn't be able to stay with her, that they'd take her from him. But they did, overriding his furious protests with the ease of long practice.

And in that moment, standing all alone in the middle of an antiseptic waiting room, Joc learned the true meaning of helplessness.

Over the space of the next two hours, Joc paced every inch of the waiting room. By the end of the first sixty minutes he'd memorized each stain on the rug and all twenty-three nicks, holes and blemishes on the walls. By the end of the second, he could have named every cookie, candy and drink item offered for sale in the vending machines. And he could have done it blindfolded.

Still no one came to give him an update on Rosalyn's status. Finally he'd had enough. He didn't care if he had to buy the damn hospital, someone was going to give him the information he needed. He started toward the door when Rosalyn's doctor appeared in the doorway.

"How is she?" Joc demanded. "Is she all right?"

"Does Ms. Oakley have any family?"

"I'm her family." He struggled to keep from shouting at the man, fought to keep his tone level. "Please. How is she?"

"She'll live. Cuts, bruises and abrasions. The concussion has us a little worried, but all the scans are clear."

"And the baby?"

The doctor checked his chart. "I gather she's very early in her pregnancy?"

"Six weeks."

"She hasn't miscarried. But there's still that risk," the doctor warned. He gestured to the nurse standing behind him. "You can see her now, if you'd like. The next few days should tell the story."

When Rosalyn came to this time, the pain wasn't anywhere near as bad as the other half dozen occasions she'd regained consciousness. This time she took note of her surroundings, realizing she lay in a hospital bed. The air smelled sharp and cold with the acrid scent of disinfectant and whatever medicines the doctors had dripping into her arm. Somewhere nearby machines beeped softly.

She struggled to focus, fighting the splitting headache that blurred her vision and made her want to retreat into oblivion. Someone had turned down the lights to dim the room, making it difficult to see clearly. But even so she could make out a familiar form holding up one of the walls of her room.

"Joc?"

He straightened at her whispered call and crossed to the bed. Muted midday sunshine filtered in from a shaded

window and gilded the hospital room with the faintest
golden glow, a glow that flowed over and around him like
a halo and gave him the appearance of a fallen angel.

"I'm here, Red."

She asked the same question she'd asked every other
time she'd awakened. "The baby? Did I lose our baby?"

And he gave her the exact same answer. "Our
baby's safe."

Tears tracked down her cheeks. "I'm sorry. I was so
upset and so angry. I forgot about the loose carpet. I've
been meaning to have it fixed for months now. If I had,
none of this would have happened."

He leaned down, feathering a gentle kiss across her
mouth. "You don't need to worry about that now."

"But I could have killed our baby." She scrubbed at
her tears with the heels of her palms, flinching when she
inadvertently hit bruised skin.

He caught her hands in his and drew them away from
her cheeks. "Let me take care of that for you. You're a
bit banged up. When you tripped, you fell against a
sideboard and it tipped over onto you. You've got the
mother of all shiners."

"I don't remember. I don't remember anything after
I tripped." He dampened a washcloth with cool water
and cleaned her face with such exquisite care that tears
flooded her eyes all over again.

"Hey, cut off the waterworks, Red," he teased with a
tenderness that stole her breath. "You're leaking faster
than I can mop up."

"Joc—" She moistened her dry lips. "What happened
with MacKenzie?"

The question caused a mask to drop over his face, one she found impossible to penetrate. "I kicked her out of the house after you were injured."

It wasn't what she meant and she suspected he knew it, knew it and was avoiding her question—which could only mean one thing. Her heart sank. "For how long?" At his silence, her desperation grew. "Does she really own Longhorn?"

"I don't know." He kept his response light, but she could see the truth in the bleakness of his gaze. "I'll have my lawyers look into it first thing tomorrow. If we can get Duff to admit that he disposed of the mortgage payments instead of mailing them and that MacKenzie paid him to do it, there's a chance we can get this turned around."

She shifted restlessly. "I can't lose my ranch. I can't."

"Right now you need to relax and give yourself time to heal." He splayed his hand across her abdomen, his touch feather-light. "Your recovery is more important than anything else."

He was right. Her health and that of their baby's came before everything else. She nodded, feeling exhaustion tugging at her again. She reached for his hand and squeezed it in acknowledgment, too tired to do more. Her eyes fluttered, then closed. "Think I'll rest now," she mumbled.

"Red?" She heard Joc's voice from a great distance. "Sweetheart? I need to tell you something. I need you to know…"

She tried to hold on, struggled to fight against the relentless drag of sleep and listen to what he was telling her. But she lost the battle and slid into a soft, gentle darkness where nothing could harm her or her baby. Where she still owned Longhorn and the man she loved stood strong and proud at her side while they raised their baby together.

Joc sat slumped in the chair beside Rosalyn's bed, shifting in a vain attempt to find a more comfortable position. Not possible, of course, not that that kept him from trying. He checked to see whether she still slept, reassured when he saw the slow, easy give in and take of her breath. It was a far more natural sleep than earlier, and a hint of color tinted the unbruised portions of her cheeks a healthy pink.

Had she heard him earlier? Had she heard him declare his love? He thought her lashes had flickered in response to the words, but he couldn't be certain. His jaw firmed. Next time she woke, they'd be the first words out of his mouth. He'd make sure of that. Restless, he pushed himself to his feet only to discover MacKenzie standing in the doorway staring at Rosalyn.

"What the hell are you doing here?" he demanded in a harsh undertone.

She was perceptive enough not to advance any farther into the room. "I had to come," she explained in a rush. "I'm so sorry, Joc. I know I'm partially responsible for the accident. How is she?"

"How is she?"

Pain howled through him and he lost it. Completely, thoroughly lost it. It was as though his brain disengaged from his body and all his senses went off-line. One minute he was in perfect control and the next he was streaking toward her, running off pure instinct and adrenaline. Maybe he would have been able to maintain some semblance of restraint if he hadn't been so exhausted or so terrified of losing everything that mattered most to him. When he came to himself, he had MacKenzie up against the wall, his hands fisted around the lapels of her blouse.

"If anything happens to her or our child, I swear to you I'll take you apart, piece by piece." His voice escaped low and guttural and filled with bone-chilling intensity. "You got me?"

"Child!" MacKenzie shook her head in stunned disbelief. "No, no. Oh God, Joc. She's pregnant? Have they said how the baby is? Is it safe?"

"So far." His jaw worked and the breath shuddered in and out of his lungs. It took endless seconds before he could gather up his self-control once again. "I'll make you pay, MacKenzie. If anything happens to Rosalyn, I swear I'll take you down."

She stiffened within his hold. "How dare you threaten me? You started this, Arnaud. You had to take the Hollister homestead. You couldn't get it through legitimate means, so you stole it away from my mother. Well, I've got news for you. You can take my home, but it still won't make you one of us."

He flinched, amazed that he still had the capacity to feel hurt after all this time. He suddenly realized he continued to hold her pinned against the wall, and with great care, opened his hands and released her. "I've kept my distance in the past out of respect for your mother." He fought to keep his voice to a mere whisper so they wouldn't disturb Rosalyn. He backed away from

MacKenzie, putting some much needed breathing distance between them. "But that ends after today. So we're clear? The gloves come off. As far as I'm concerned, we're no longer family. Hell, you never wanted to be, anyway."

"Do your worst, Joc, but it won't get you Rosalyn's ranch." She yanked at her blouse and straightened the crushed collar. "Only I can give you what you want."

That gave him pause. "Don't play games with me. Are you willing to sell Longhorn to me, or not?"

"Oh, I'm willing."

Now for the vital question. "How much do you want for it?" As far as he was concerned, everything and anything was on the table so long as it didn't adversely impact Rosalyn and their baby.

She stared at him with eyes that had haunted him all his life, eyes he wanted to hate. His father's eyes. But the pain that filled MacKenzie's were far different from any expression he'd ever seen in Boss Hollister's. The expression he read there was one he'd seen all too often, and always in the same place.

In his own mirror.

"I don't want your money." Her mouth quivered for an instant before she firmed it. "I want the Hollister homestead. I'll trade it for Longhorn."

He swore beneath his breath. He should have seen it coming. Maybe if he hadn't been so distracted by Rosalyn and the baby he would have. MacKenzie's offer left him wanting to howl in fury. "That's the one thing I can't give you. Name anything else, MacKenzie. I'll pay any amount you want."

Tears of fury glistened in her eyes and she trembled visibly in an effort to control them. "I don't want money, damn you! I want my home."

"I can't."

"Fine. Don't make the deal. I'll leave you to explain to your fiancée—" Her glance flickered in Rosalyn's direction. "Or maybe that's now your ex-fiancée—why you refused to save her home from my bulldozers. Something tells me you're not going to have much success."

Joc spun around. Rosalyn lay there, her eyes a violent blue and filled with heart-breaking disillusionment.

"Why?" Rosalyn asked. She couldn't believe what she'd overheard. "You have it within your power to save Longhorn and you won't do it. Why?"

He held his position on the far side of the room, distancing himself from her. The instant he realized she was awake and had overheard his conversation with MacKenzie, his face had fallen into impenetrable lines, giving nothing away. "I'm sorry, Red. I can't do it, and I can't explain why."

"Can't...or won't?"

"Take your pick."

She didn't understand it. Didn't understand his attitude. Didn't understand his remoteness. This man bore no resemblance to the one she'd fallen in love with, the one she could have sworn had declared his love for her. She tried again, desperate to break through the barriers he'd thrown up. "You told me that your father's land held no importance to you. That you weren't trying to reconnect with him through his homestead."

"I'm not."

"Then why—"

He simply shook his head.

She believed him, at least on that front. He'd been too adamant on that subject. If he'd been lying to her, or even to himself, she'd have picked up on that by now. She scrambled for another explanation. "Is it revenge? Is that it? Is this your way of hitting back at the Hollisters? Is getting even for what Boss did to you still so important after all these years?"

"Would you believe me if I said no?"

She shook her head, wincing at the pain pounding between her temples. "I don't know what to believe anymore. And you won't explain. What am I supposed to think?"

He approached then, sliding a hip onto the edge of her bed. "I need you to trust me, Red."

"You've asked that of me again and again. And each time I have." She swept tears from her cheeks, the jarring contact with her bruises making her flinch. "But you have the ability to save my property and you refuse to do it. Is hanging on to your father's land that important to you?"

"All I can tell you is that I have a good reason for my actions."

Another possibility occurred to her, one that broke her heart. "Was MacKenzie right? Is this all a game to the two of you?"

He hesitated. "Until now, I suppose it has been some sort of game."

"Well, this isn't a game to me. It's my life!"

"Listen to me, Red. MacKenzie despises my existence. It doesn't matter that I had nothing to do with the circumstances surrounding my birth, or that Ana and I are as much a victim of Boss's callousness as MacKenzie and her brothers. She's intent on besting me. And she doesn't care who gets in the way or how badly they're hurt, so long as she wins."

"But you can put an end to it. It's within your power." She couldn't keep the desperation from her voice. "All you have to do is give her what she wants. Or is the win as important to you as it is to her?"

He replied with painful gentleness. "I'll tell you what I told her. Ask me for anything else, anything at all, and it's yours. Despite what you think, this is the one thing it's not in my power to give you." He searched her expression and his mouth compressed. "You won't be able to forgive me if I don't make the trade, will you? It will always stand between us."

She wanted to deny it, wished she could be generous enough to shrug off the loss and move on with her life. But she'd been the sole protector of Longhorn for too many years to do that. It was her only connection with her parents and the generations of Oakleys before them. Her chin quivered, her silence condemning her.

He stood. "I'll be back tomorrow. We'll talk more then."

"Don't come," she whispered. "There's nothing left to be said."

He hesitated, then inclined his head. Without another word, he walked out of the room.

The instant Joc left, Rosalyn leaned back against her pillows and closed her eyes, fighting a resurgence of tears. Something was terribly wrong. She didn't know what, but every instinct warned of it. She had a horrible feeling the problem extended beyond the situation with her ranch and the Hollister homestead. But for the life of her she couldn't figure it out. And unless Joc trusted her enough to tell her the truth, she doubted she ever would.

Her hand stole across her belly. What would have happened between them if she'd miscarried the baby? Or if she hadn't trusted Duff with mailing her loan payments and still owned the ranch? Would Joc still be insisting on marriage?

How could she make a rational decision from this point forward if he wouldn't talk to her about whatever secret he was keeping? How could they have a successful marriage if he shut her out?

Or if he was marrying her for all the wrong reasons?

The door to her room thrust open and for a split second she thought it might be Joc. That he'd returned to tell her he'd made a terrible mistake and that he'd do whatever necessary to save Longhorn. Instead a nurse entered to check on Rosalyn's vital statistics.

Why hadn't he been willing to trade Longhorn for MacKenzie's old home? The question nagged at her. The only reason she could think of was the one reason she most wanted to deny. He hadn't been willing to make the trade because doing so would force her and their baby to live in his world instead of on the ranch. That it would give him the control he'd lose by agreeing to her stipulation about marriage. Could he be that ruthless? She rubbed her aching head. Who was she kidding?

Joc had invented the word.

* * *

It was past midnight when Joc placed the call. A sleepy voice answered on the fifth ring.

"It's Arnaud," he announced. "We have a problem."

"Do you realize what time it is?"

"I'm well aware of the time." His hand bunched into a fist. "I need your help, Meredith."

There was a long moment of silence. "I would have thought I'd helped you quite enough."

He let that slide. "MacKenzie managed to get her hands on Rosalyn's ranch. She's going to raze it if I don't trade your old place for Longhorn. You need to stop her."

"Oh God. I'll speak to her, but I doubt it'll do any good."

He fought to remain calm. Never before had self-control been an issue. But it was an issue tonight. "You can do more than speak to her," he insisted.

There was a moment of silence, then, "We've had this conversation before. You made a promise to me and I expect you to keep your word."

He closed his eyes. "Do you doubt I will?"

"You made a commitment to Ana that you'd change your life when you were a twenty-year-old hoodlum. To the best of my knowledge, you haven't broken your word since then. I assume you're not going to start now?"

"No."

Relief bled through her words. "I'll do what I can, but MacKenzie can be as stubborn as you when it comes to certain issues."

"I can't lose her, Meredith," he whispered. "Not Rosalyn. Anything but her."

"You love her?" she asked, shocked. "You, Joc?"

"More than anything. That ranch means everything to her." He fought to speak through the thickness clogging his throat. "Even more than me."

"Okay, I'll do what I can."

Ten

Thirty-six hours later, Rosalyn checked herself out of the hospital. Her doctors weren't happy, particularly when they learned that Joc wouldn't be picking her up. But then, how could he when she'd neglected to call him? Since both she and the baby were fully recovered, they reluctantly agreed to discharge her.

Exiting through the front doors, she took a deep breath. She might be inhaling city air rather than air sweetened with the grass and flowers and ripening grains of home, but at least it was better than a hospital room scented with the harsh odor of bleach and illness. Now she just had to decide where to go next.

Joc's place was out. She needed time to deal with all that had happened between them before confronting him again. She could return to Longhorn—it was hers for a few days more at least. But did she want to go back there? Before she could decide what her next move would be, a sleek black car drove into the entry circle and pulled to a stop in front of her.

The passenger door swung open and a woman called out to her. "Ms. Oakley…Rosalyn? I arranged with your housekeeper, Claire, to pick you up."

Rosalyn blinked in surprise, cautiously approaching the car. "I'm sorry. Do I know you?"

"Indirectly, my dear. I'm Meredith Hollister. I think we need to talk."

Rosalyn made a snap decision and slid into the car, studying Meredith with interest. The woman appeared to be in her forties, despite the fact that basic math put her somewhere in her fifties. She was also every bit as striking as her daughter, although their appearances couldn't be more disparate. Where MacKenzie shared her half brother's height, and eye-catching, dark looks, Meredith was a small, sleek package with a cap of streaked blond curls and a lovely, fine-boned face.

"How did you know I was being discharged at this moment?" Rosalyn asked, genuinely curious. "Joc didn't even know."

Meredith dismissed that with a wave of her mani-cured hand. To Rosalyn's surprise her fingernails were simple, polished ovals. Practical rather than flashy. "I bribed one of your nurses to give me the heads-up. Then I called your housekeeper and offered to take you where you needed to go."

"I'm not sure what we have to talk about." Rosalyn snapped her seat belt in place, wincing at the protest of still-tender muscles. "But I appreciate the ride."

"I thought we could talk about Joc."

The comment was so unexpected Rosalyn didn't know what to say. "You want to talk to me about Joc?" she offered hesitantly. "That can't be good."

Meredith shot her a sparkling look, one filled with good humor. "Why would you think that? I admire Joc immensely." She pulled away from the hospital. "Where can I take you?"

"I guess I'll settle for home. Unfortunately it won't be mine for much longer," Rosalyn answered, hoping she didn't sound too pathetic.

"Ah. You're referring to MacKenzie. My daughter doesn't play fair."

That provoked a spurt of temper. "She bribed one of my hands to tear up my mortgage payments. Since she held the loan on my place, it allowed her to foreclose on it. So, you're right. She doesn't play fair."

"She wants her home back. She thought Joc would trade."

"I don't hold that against her. I understand all about roots. What I object to is how she went about getting her way, and that she used me to get at Joc."

Meredith frowned in concern. "You're getting worked up about it. That can't be healthy. Why don't you put your seat back and rest? I expect the drive to take a while."

"I'm not really tired—"

"You left the hospital before they wanted to release you. Consider the health of your baby, if nothing else."

Every last protest vanished beneath the logic of that one statement. When it came to pushing buttons, this woman was good. Grumbling beneath her breath, Rosalyn reclined the seat and closed her eyes. She didn't actually nod off. Instead she lay in that dreamy world somewhere between consciousness and sleep. It wasn't until the car slowed that she sat up again. They turned onto a long, sweeping driveway, one that was all-too familiar. Rosalyn stared in dismay as they approached Joc's mansion.

"What are you doing? I didn't want to come here."

"Didn't you? Oops. My mistake. I thought you said you wanted to go home."

"This isn't my home."

"Huh. I thought it was." Meredith pulled to a stop at the base of the broad, shallow staircase that led to Joc's massive front entryway. "Would you mind if I offer you some advice?"

"I'd rather you didn't," Rosalyn answered truthfully.

"I understand. But I think I will, anyway." Fine lines spiked outward from the older woman's mouth and eyes, lines that spoke of an old, bitter pain. "I've learned the hard way that when we lose the things that are most important to us, we can become angry and cynical. Or we can find a way to take what we have left and make the best of it. You're facing that choice now. Joc loves you, you know."

"That's not true—"

Meredith cut her off. "It is true, just as it's true that you love him. You have a choice, Rosalyn. You can either put the past behind you and create a new life with the man you love, or you can use what's happened as an excuse to shut yourself off from happiness. When I was faced with a similar dilemma, I made the wrong choice. So has most of my family." She held Rosalyn with a gaze both pleading and commanding. "Don't do that to Joc. He deserves better."

Rosalyn stared in disbelief. "How can you defend him? He's taken everything from you."

"You're wrong. Boss did, not Joc." Her chin firmed and she nodded as though in response to some private decision. "Do me a favor, won't you? Tell Joc I'm releasing him from his promise. He'll know what I mean."

Rosalyn remained where she was for several long minutes, before releasing her breath in a sigh. "You're going to sit here until I get out, aren't you?"

"'Fraid so." She wiggled her fingers in the direction of the front door. "Off you go, my dear. And don't forget to give Joc my message."

Rosalyn thrust open the door and exited into a blanket of stifling humidity. Without a backward look, she trotted up the steps and entered Joc's home. She walked into blessed coolness, her advent startling one of the maids who greeted her with a smile of delight.

"Ms. Rosalyn, welcome home."

"Thanks, Lynn. Do you know where Joc is?"

"In his study."

Rosalyn's stomach knotted. She didn't want to confront Joc again, not after how they'd last parted. But she didn't have any choice. Meredith had seen to that.

The door to the study was closed and she paused outside, her fist raised to knock. Meredith's words continued to haunt her, and her arm fell to her side as she took a moment to gather up her self-control.

Meredith was right. She did have a decision to make before she saw Joc again. She could hate him for refusing MacKenzie's offer, could spend the rest of her life resenting what had happened. Or she could accept responsibility for her part in the disaster and move on. If she'd kept her bank accounts reconciled she might have realized in time that her mortgage checks weren't being cashed and put an end to MacKenzie's scheme before it had a chance to get off the ground.

More to the point, Joc had no obligation to use his assets to save Longhorn. A hard realization struck. Good Lord! If he had bailed her out, he'd own the property, not her. And he'd be within his rights to build the complex he wanted, rather than keep her ranch intact. Why hadn't that occurred to her before? Perhaps it had been the knock to her head or the medications she'd been given. Whatever the cause, she hadn't been thinking straight.

She pressed a hand to her abdomen. Boss had caused so much strife and turmoil, putting his own selfish desires before his wife and children, not to mention Joc's mother. It would be such an easy path for her to take, as well, a path of bitterness and emotional dearth. Or she could trust Joc, trust that he'd do everything within his power to care for her and their child. And maybe in time, Meredith's claim that Joc loved her might come true.

Closing her eyes, Rosalyn made her peace with the

past and with all she'd lost. From now on, she'd focus
on the future and on the life she wanted to create for her
child. It was time to provide a new legacy for the next
generation. From this point forward, she'd put down
new roots. She straightened and knocked on the heavy
oak.

"I told you I didn't want to be interrupted!"

She thrust open the door. "Too bad, Arnaud. I'm here
and you're going to have to deal with me."

"Red!" He shot to his feet, his drink sloshing over the
rim of his tumbler. "Are you all right? The baby?"

"Mother and baby are both fine, thanks."

She studied him, secretly shocked by his condition.
Though it had only been days since she'd last seen him,
he looked as though he hadn't slept in a month. Deep
lines bracketed his mouth. But it was his eyes that held
her, eyes that were bottomless wells of pain.

"I was told you wouldn't be released until tomorrow."
He circled the desk. He started to reach for her, his arms
dropping to his sides at the last instant, as though he
were afraid to touch her. "Why didn't you call me? I
would have come and picked you up."

"I didn't want to see you."

He stiffened at that. "Then why are you here?"

"Not out of choice, at least not at first. Meredith
drove me out here."

His face darkened. "How did she know to pick you up?"

"Apparently bribery and deception run in the Hollister family. Meredith paid one of the nurses to alert her
when I left the hospital." She stepped past him and

wandered deeper into the study, before spinning to face him once again. "She had a message for you, by the way."

Every scrap of expression vanished from his face. "What message?"

Interesting reaction. She studied him more closely. "She said she releases you from your promise. You're supposed to know what that means."

"That's all she told you?"

"Yes." She'd wasted enough time on the Hollisters. "Could we talk? I mean, really talk."

"I think that would be a good idea."

Rosalyn lifted an eyebrow. "Mind if I go first?"

He visibly steeled himself. "Go ahead."

With luck he'd understand where she was going with her request. Only one question remained…how he'd react to it. "I'd like to renegotiate our agreement, the one regarding the baby and our marriage."

She'd intrigued him, though he still remained wary. "Which particular clause?"

"The one that determines where we live."

A muscle leaped in his jaw and his gaze intensified, filled with desperate hope. "I think I'd be open to a change in venue. Where do you have in mind?"

"Wherever you're willing to put down roots. Wherever we can put those roots down together," she said simply. "If you're willing, that is."

He came for her then, catching her close. "Warn me if I hurt you."

She shut her eyes and leaned into him. "I've discovered that I can handle a little hurt. I bounce back fast."

"Are you sure, Red? Really sure?"

Her head jerked up and she regarded him with un-flinching certainty. "Absolutely. It doesn't matter if MacKenzie owns Longhorn now. It's dirt, remember? Nothing more than acres of dirt."

He stilled against her and his breath escaped in a long sigh. "I seem to remember saying those words to you when we were on Deseos." A hint of regret drifted across his face. "They were wrong then and they're wrong now."

She pulled back. "What do you mean?"

"I mean I plan to fix it."

She shook her head. "No, you don't need to do that. It doesn't matter where we live." Didn't he get it? She took his hand in hers and placed it low on her abdomen. "Nothing matters except us and our child. We're Texans. They don't grow them any tougher. We can plant our roots anywhere."

"And we will. We'll plant them on Oakley land."

Rosalyn stared in disbelief. "MacKenzie changed her mind?"

"She will."

He swung her into his arms, and with the utmost caution, carried her to the leather couch on the far side of his study. "I don't dare take you upstairs," he said with clear regret. "I'm not sure I could keep my hands off you and you need time to heal."

"Fortunately for us both, I'm a fast healer."

As though unable to help himself he kissed her, his mouth brushing hers with the lightest of touches. It wasn't enough—nowhere near enough. She lifted her mouth for another. With a husky groan he kissed her again, sealing her mouth with his. He delved gently inward, slow and careful and infinitely tender.

"More," she demanded the minute he lifted his head.

"Your bruises…"

"You can kiss them better." She shot him a humorous glance. "It'll be good practice for when the baby's born."

He didn't need any further prompting. He settled back against the cushions and with exquisite sensitivity, helped her stretch out on top of him. "Are you all right?"

"Perfect."

The next several minutes passed in a delicious haze. Her enjoyment of being in his arms again overrode any discomfort she might have experienced from her injuries. His kisses were sweeter than any that had come before, telling her without words all that lay within his heart. Every touch felt soft and slow and keenly aware of how they might impact her injuries. Desire rose like a tide, threatening to spiral out of control. Suddenly he pulled back.

"No more," he insisted, the breath heaving from his lungs. "Not until your doctor gives us the okay."

Realizing that she didn't have a hope of changing his mind, she raised her head and regarded him with undisguised curiosity. "Explain it to me, Joc. Why will MacKenzie sell Longhorn to you? What's changed over the past few days?"

"Meredith happened."

"The promise?" At his nod, she asked, "What promise did you make to her?"

"That I'd never tell anyone why she sold her home to me. And that I'd never sell it without her permission."

"I don't understand," she said in bewilderment.

"Meredith approached me not long after I made my first million—maybe a decade ago. She begged me to buy the property."

She stared, dumbfounded. "Why would she do that?"

"Because she was on the verge of bankruptcy. Between Boss's legal fees and the taxes and fines that resulted from his illegal activities, there was nothing left."

The pieces started to fall into place. "MacKenzie doesn't know any of this, does she?"

Joc shook his head. "No. Nor do her brothers. Meredith didn't want them to know. Pride, I suspect. She split the money among them and claimed it was their inheritance from their father."

"Why did she want you to hold on to the property?"

"I think she has mixed feelings about it. Part of her hates the place because of Boss. Part of her is torn because the homestead has been in Hollister hands for so many years. She felt that as long as I held on to it, she had time to come to terms with her feelings and to decide what she wanted done with it."

Rosalyn blinked in surprise. "I don't get it. Why would you let her make that decision?"

"It was part of our agreement. Since I didn't care what happened to the place, the stipulation didn't bother me. The one thing Meredith has remained adamant about is not passing the homestead on to her children. She didn't want them continuing a legacy that brought them nothing but pain."

"Which is why she didn't want you selling it to Mac-Kenzie, even a decade later." Rosalyn frowned. "Why did she want it after all this time?"

"MacKenzie found out a year ago that I—or rather, one of my corporations—owns the property. She can't stand it and has been after me ever since to sell out to her."

Rosalyn needed to put another issue to rest. "Are you positive you don't want it for yourself?"

Bone-deep anger burned in his eyes. "I've never set foot on Boss's land and I never will."

"What do you think Meredith will do with it?"

"We've discussed turning it into a camp for children suffering from life-threatening diseases, or perhaps a rehabilitation center for troubled teens."

"Are you going to tell MacKenzie the truth?"

He nodded. "I'll arrange a meeting with her and Meredith and see if she won't come on board with her mother's plans. I have a feeling she will, and that once she understands why I refused to sell it to her, she'll allow me to purchase Longhorn." His mouth twisted. "Knowing her, it'll be for a hefty price."

"Why, Joc?" she asked softly. "Why would you do that for your mother's nemesis?"

"Because she saved my life."

Rosalyn lifted onto one elbow. *"What?"*

"It was during that time when I was trying to change

my life around. When I put an end to my more questionable business enterprises—"

"That's a tactful way of putting it."

"I thought so." His smile held a hint of pain. "There wasn't any money coming in once I parted ways with Mick and the others. And I still had the responsibility for Ana."

The penny dropped. "Harvard. Meredith paid for you to go to Harvard, didn't she?"

He shook his head. "Money was tight for her, too. No, she didn't pay for it. But she found people who could. At Meredith's urging, they took a chance on me. They supported me while I got my education and during the years I was getting my business off the ground."

"For which they've since been richly rewarded," Rosalyn guessed shrewdly.

He shrugged. "I've been in a position to help a few of them," he admitted. "Meredith also arranged for references from people who had an in at Harvard. And she arranged for housing, housing that enabled me to keep Ana with me during those early years."

"So much," Rosalyn marveled. "Why would she do all that?"

"Because she understood that Ana and I were the innocent ones, the ones who suffered the most, even more than her own children. Meredith is…she's quite a lady. After what she did for me, how could I refuse her request when she was in trouble?"

"You couldn't."

"She even tried to reconcile the differences between her children, and Ana and me."

"Without success."

He grimaced. "Her attempts only made matters worse. MacKenzie, in particular, resented her mother's interference. She's always thought I had some hold over Meredith, that I put pressure on her. It never occurred to her that it was the other way around."

They lay in silent accord for a long time after that while Rosalyn worked up the nerve to ask her final question. Unable to stand it any longer, she cleared her throat. "Meredith told me something else."

"Meredith's been busy," Joc said drily. "What else did she say?"

"She claimed you loved me." Rosalyn peeked up at him. "Was she right, Joc? Do you love me?"

The tenderness in his expression said it all. "How can you doubt it?" He slid his fingers deep into her hair and tugged her down until their mouths collided. And then he removed all doubts, giving of himself without holding anything back. When she'd melted into a helpless puddle, he released her with a slow grin. "I love you with every fiber of my being, and I always will. Any other questions?"

"Just one. What happens if MacKenzie sells you Longhorn?"

His brows tugged together. "We move in, of course. That's what we agreed, isn't it?"

"But your complex…"

Understanding dawned. "Ah. You're wondering if I won't decide to build my office complex if I end up owning Longhorn."

"It's just that there are a lot of roots on my ranch." She hastened to correct herself. "Your ranch."

"*Our* ranch, Red."

"Our ranch," she repeated. A gentle unloosening swept over her at the word, even as she issued a warning. "You might find those roots trip you up, if you're not careful."

"They can't trip you if your own roots are tangled up there, too. And they are. They're tangled so tightly with yours that they'll never pull loose. And with all those roots cluttering up the place it certainly makes the property inappropriate for anything other than ranching." He kissed away her tears of joy before sliding his hand across her belly in a gesture that had become heartwarmingly familiar. "I have some suggestions for names."

She laughed through her tears. "Already?"

"I had a lot of time to think over the past couple days." He hesitated, revealing an uncertainty that sat oddly on his face. "If it's a boy, how does the name Joshua appeal to you?"

The tears intensified and she had trouble responding. "That—that was the name of my brother."

"Yes, I know. I saw it at the cemetery."

"Thank you. It would mean a lot to name our son after my brother." It took her a moment to regain her control. "Joc?"

"Yes, Red?"

"I love you."

"That's all that's important." He lowered his head, and with infinite care, kissed her.

As Rosalyn surrendered to Joc's embrace, she knew deep in her heart that their child would be a boy. A boy named Joshua with hair as black as ebony and eyes the exact same shade as Texas Bluebonnets. A boy who'd grow tall and strong and broad. A boy who would provide the trunk for a tree that would send out endless branches, each growing large and full, nourished by the roots from which he sprang.

Roots that ran deep into Texan soil.

* * * * *

Don't miss Day Leclaire's new series for Silhouette Desire, THE DANTE LEGACY, launching February 2008

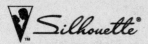

Romantic
SUSPENSE

Sparked by Danger,
Fueled by Passion.

When evidence is found that Mallory Dawes intends to sell the personal financial information of government employees to "the Russian," OMEGA engages undercover agent Cutter Smith. Tailing her all the way to France, Cutter is fighting a growing attraction to Mallory while at the same time having to determine her connection to "the Russian." Is Mallory really the mouse in this game of cat and mouse?

Look for

Stranded with a Spy

by *USA TODAY* bestselling author

Merline Lovelace

October 2007.

Also available October wherever you buy books:

BULLETPROOF MARRIAGE *(Mission: Impassioned)*
by Karen Whiddon

A HERO'S REDEMPTION *(Haven)* by Suzanne McMinn

TOUCHED BY FIRE by Elizabeth Sinclair

Ria Sterling has the gift—or is it a curse?—
of seeing a person's future in his or her
photograph. Unfortunately, when detective
Carrick Jones brings her a missing person's
case, she glimpses his partner's ID—and
sees imminent murder. And when her vision
comes true, Ria becomes the prime suspect.
Carrick isn't convinced this beautiful woman
committed the crime...but does he believe
she has the special powers to solve it?

Look for

Seeing Is Believing

by

Kate Austin

Available October
wherever you buy books.

REQUEST YOUR FREE BOOKS!

2 FREE NOVELS PLUS 2 FREE GIFTS!

Passionate, Powerful, Provocative!

Mediterranean
N I G H T S™

*Sail aboard the luxurious Alexandra's Dream and
experience glamour, romance, mystery and revenge!*

Coming in October 2007...

AN AFFAIR TO
REMEMBER

by

Karen Kendall

When Captain Nikolas Pappas first fell in love with
Helena Stamos, he was a penniless deckhand and she
was the daughter of a shipping magnate. But he's
never forgiven himself for the way he left her—and
fifteen years later, he's determined to win her back.

Though the attraction is still there, Helena is hesitant
to get involved. Nick left her once...what's to stop
him from doing it again?

Silhouette
Desire

There was only one man for the job—
an impossible-to-resist maverick
she knew she didn't dare fall for.

MAVERICK
(#1827)

BY *NEW YORK TIMES*
BESTSELLING AUTHOR
JOAN HOHL

"Will You Do It for One Million Dollars?"

Any other time, Tanner Wolfe would have balked at being
hired by a woman. Yet Brianna Stewart was desperate to
engage the infamous bounty hunter. The price was just
high enough to gain Tanner's interest…Brianna's beauty
definitely strong enough to keep it. But he wasn't about
to allow her to tag along on his mission. He worked
alone. Always had. Always would. However, he'd never
confronted a more determined client than Brianna. She
wasn't taking no for an answer—not about anything.

Perhaps a million-dollar bounty was not the only thing
this maverick was about to gain….

Look for MAVERICK

Available October 2007 wherever you buy books.

COMING NEXT MONTH

**#1825 STRANDED WITH THE TEMPTING STRANGER—
Brenda Jackson**
The Garrisons
He began his seduction with secrets and scandals in mind...but
bedding the Garrison heiress could lead to the ultimate downfall
of his hardened heart.

**#1826 CAPTURED BY THE BILLIONAIRE—
Maureen Child**
Reasons for Revenge
Trapped on an island resort with the man she had once jilted, she
knew her billionaire captor was about to teach her a lesson she'd
never forget.

**#1827 MAVERICK—*New York Times* bestselling author
Joan Hohl**
There was only one man for the job—an impossible-to-resist
maverick she didn't dare fall for.

**#1828 MILLIONAIRE'S CALCULATED BABY BID—
Laura Wright**
No Ring Required
She agreed to produce an heir to his financial empire...but the
secret behind this baby bargain could threaten more than their
growing attraction to one another.

**#1829 THE APOLLONIDES MISTRESS SCANDAL—
Tessa Radley**
Billionaire Heirs
Posing as her identical twin, she vowed revenge against her sister's
Greek lover...until she became caught in his web of seduction.

**#1830 SEDUCED FOR THE INHERITANCE—
Jennifer Lewis**
He would do anything to keep her from claiming his family's
inheritance...even if it meant sleeping with the one woman he
shouldn't desire....

SDCNM0907